WOULD YOU WANT YOUR SISTER
TO MARRY A CHINGER?

It was the highest honor to defend the Empire against the dreaded Chingers, an enemy race of seven-foot-tall lizardoids.

But Bill, who hailed from a hickworld of peaceful farmers, soon discovers that war is hell when he is shanghaied into the galactic navy.

From the sweltering fuse room aboard the *Christine Keeler*, where he loses an arm while blasting a Chinger spaceship, to the Department of Sanitation far below the world-city of Helior, where he finds peace, job security, and unlimited trash ... here is Bill, a pure-hearted fool fighting a deluxe cast of robots, androids, and aliens in a never-ending losing battle to preserve his humanity while upholding the glory of the Empire.

BILL THE GALACTIC HERO

HARRY HARRISON

AVON BOOKS ◆ NEW YORK

All of the characters in this book are fictitious, and any resemblance to actual persons, living or dead, is purely coincidental and, besides, they aren't even born yet.

AVON BOOKS
A division of
The Hearst Corporation
105 Madison Avenue
New York, New York 10016

Copyright © 1965 by Harry Harrison
Front cover illustration by Michael W. Kaluta and Steve Fastner
Published by arrangement with the author
Library of Congress Catalog Card Number: 65-11622
ISBN: 0-380-00395-3

First Avon Books Mass Market Printing: November 1979
First Avon Books Trade Printing: August 1975

AVON TRADEMARK REG. U.S. PAT. OFF. AND IN OTHER COUNTRIES, MARCA REGISTRADA, HECHO EN U.S.A.

Printed in the U.S.A.

OPM   10 9 8 7 6 5

For my shipmate
BRIAN W. ALDISS
who is reading the sextant
and plotting the course
for us all.

I

Bill never realized that sex was the cause of it all. If the sun that morning had not been burning so warmly in the brassy sky of Phigerinadon II, and if he had not glimpsed the sugar-white and wine-barrel-wide backside of Inga-Maria Calyphigia while she bathed in the stream, he might have paid more attention to his plowing than to the burning pressures of heterosexuality and would have driven his furrow to the far side of the hill before the seductive music sounded along the road. He might never have heard it, and his life would have been very, very different. But he did hear it and dropped the handles of the plow that was plugged into the robomule, turned, and gaped.

It was indeed a fabulous sight. Leading the parade was a one-robot band, twelve feet high and splendid in its great black busby that concealed the hi-fi speakers. The golden pillars of its legs stamped forward as its thirty articulated arms sawed, plucked, and fingered at a dazzling variety of instruments. Martial music poured out in wave after inspiring wave, and even Bill's thick peasant feet stirred in their clodhoppers as the shining boots of the squad of soldiers crashed along the road in perfect unison. Medals jingled on the manly swell of their scarlet-clad chests, and there could certainly be no nobler sight in all the world. To their rear marched the sergeant, gorgeous in his braid and brass, thickly clustered medals and ribbons, sword and gun, girdled gut and steely eye which sought out Bill where he stood gawking over the fence. The grizzled head nodded in his direction, the steel-trap mouth bent into a friendly smile and there was a conspiratorial wink. Then the little legion was past, and hurrying behind in their wake came a huddle of dust-covered ancillary robots, hopping and crawling or rippling along on treads. As soon as these had gone by Bill climbed clumsily over the split-rail fence and ran after them. There were no more than two interesting events every four years here, and he was not going to miss what promised to be a third.

A crowd had already gathered in the market square when Bill hurried up, and they were listening to an enthusiastic band concert. The robot hurled itself into the glorious measures of "Star Troopers to the Skies Avaunt," thrashed its way through "Rockets Rumble," and almost demolished itself in the tumultuous rhythm of "Sappers at the Pithead Digging." It pursued this last tune so strenuously that one of its legs flew off, rising high into the air, but was caught dexterously before it could hit the ground, and the music ended with the robot balancing on its remaining leg, beating time with the detached limb. It also, after an ear-fracturing peal on the basses, used the leg to point across the square to where a tri-di screen and refreshment booth had been set up. The troopers had vanished into the tavern, and the recruiting sergeant stood alone among his robots, beaming a welcoming smile.

"Now hear this! Free drinks for all, courtesy of the Emperor, and some lively scenes of jolly adventure in distant climes to amuse you while you sip," he called in an immense and leathery voice.

Most of the people drifted over, Bill in their midst, though a few embittered and elderly draft-dodgers slunk away between the houses. Cooling drinks were shared out by a robot with a spigot for a navel and an inexhaustible supply of plastic glasses in one hip. Bill sipped his happily while he followed the enthralling adventures of the space troopers in full color, with sound effects and stimulating subsonics. There was battle and death and glory, though it was only the Chingers who died: troopers only suffered neat little wounds in their extremities that could be covered easily by small bandages. And while Bill was enjoying this, Recruiting Sergeant Grue was enjoying him, his little piggy eyes ruddy with greed as they fastened onto the back of Bill's neck.

This is the one! he chortled to himself while, unknowingly, his yellowed tongue licked at his lips. He could already feel the weight of the bonus money in his pocket. The rest of the audience were the usual mixed bag of overage men, fat women, beardless youths, and other unenlistables. All except this broad-shouldered, square-chinned, curly-haired chunk of electronic-cannon fodder. With a precise hand on the controls the sergeant lowered the background subsonics and aimed a tight-beam stimulator at the back of his victim's head. Bill writhed in his seat, almost taking part in the glorious battles unfolding before him.

As the last chord died and the screen went blank, the refreshment robot pounded hollowly on its metallic chest and bellowed, "DRINK! DRINK! DRINK!" The sheeplike audience swept that way, all except Bill, who was plucked from their midst by a powerful arm.

"Here, I saved some for you," the sergeant said, passing over a prepared cup so loaded with dissolved ego-reducing drugs that they were crystallizing out at the bottom. "You're a fine figure of a lad and to my eye seem a cut above the yokels here. Did you ever think of making your career in the forces?"

"I'm not the military type, Shargeant . . ." Bill chomped his jaws and spat to remove the impediment to his speech and puzzled at the sudden fogginess in his thoughts. Though it was a tribute to his physique that he was even conscious after the volume of drugs and sonics that he had been plied

3

with. "Not the military type. My fondest ambition is to be of help in the best way I can, in my chosen career as a Technical Fertilizer Operator, and I'm almost finished with my correspondence course . . ."

"That's a crappy job for a bright lad like you," the sergeant said, while clapping him on the arm to get a good feel of his biceps. Rock. He resisted the impulse to pull Bill's lip down and take a quick peek at the condition of his back teeth. Later. "Leave that kind of job to those that like it. No chance of promotion. While a career in the troopers has no top. Why, Grand-Admiral Pflunger came up through the rocket tubes, as they say, from recruit trooper to grand-admiral. How does that sound?"

"It sounds very nice for Mr. Pflunger, but I think fertilizer operating is more fun. Gee—I'm feeling sleepy. I think I'll go lie down."

"Not before you've seen this, just as a favor to me of course," the sergeant said, cutting in front of him and pointing to a large book held open by a tiny robot. "Clothes make the man, and most men would be ashamed to be seen in a crummy-looking smock like that thing draped around you or wearing those broken canal boats on their feet. Why look like *that* when you can look like *this?*"

Bill's eyes followed the thick finger to the color plate in the book where a miracle of misapplied engineering caused his own face to appear on the illustrated figure dressed in trooper red. The sergeant flipped the pages, and on each plate the uniform was a little more gaudy, the rank higher. The last one was that of a grand-admiral, and Bill blinked at his own face under the plumed helmet, now with a touch of crow's-feet about the eyes and sporting a handsome and gray-shot mustache, but still undeniably his own.

"That's the way you will look," the sergeant murmured into his ear, "once you have climbed the ladder of success. Would

4

you like to try a uniform on? Of course you would like to try a uniform on. Tailor!"

When Bill opened his mouth to protest the sergeant put a large cigar into it, and before he could get it out the robot tailor had rolled up, swept a curtain-bearing arm about him and stripped him naked. "Hey! Hey!" he said.

"It won't hurt," the sergeant said, poking his great head through the curtain and beaming at Bill's muscled form. He poked a finger into a pectoral (rock), then withdrew.

"Ouch!" Bill said, as the tailor extruded a cold pointer and jabbed him with it, measuring his size. Something went *chunk* deep inside its tubular torso, and a brilliant red jacket began to emerge from a slot in the front. In an instant this was slipped onto Bill and the shining golden buttons buttoned. Luxurious gray moleskin trousers were pulled on next, then gleaming black knee-length boots. Bill staggered a bit as the curtain was whipped away and a powered full-length mirror rolled up.

"Oh, how the girls love a uniform," the sergeant said, "and I can't blame them."

A memory of the vision of Inga-Maria Calyphigia's matched white moons obscured Bill's sight for a moment, and when it had cleared he found he was grasping a stylo and was about to sign the form that the recruiting sergeant held before him.

"No," Bill said, a little amazed at his own firmness of mind. "I don't really want to. Technical Fertilizer Operator . . ."

"And not only will you receive this lovely uniform, an enlistment bonus, and a free medical examination, but you will be awarded these handsome medals." The sergeant took a flat box, offered to him on cue by a robot, and opened it to display a glittering array of ribbons and bangles. "This is the Honorable Enlistment Award," he intoned gravely, pinning a jewel-encrusted nebula, pendant on chartreuse, to Bill's wide chest. "And the Emperor's Congratulatory Gilded Horn, the Forward to Victory Starburst, the Praise Be Given Salutation of the Mothers of the Victorious Fallen, and the Everflowing Cornucopia which does not mean anything but looks nice and can be used to carry contraceptives." He stepped back and admired Bill's chest, which was now adangle with ribbons, shining metal, and gleaming paste gems.

"I just couldn't," Bill said. "Thank you anyway for the offer, but . . ."

The sergeant smiled, prepared even for this eleventh-hour resistance, and pressed the button on his belt that actuated the programed hypno-coil in the heel of Bill's new boot. The powerful neural current surged through the contacts and Bill's hand twitched and jumped, and when the momentary fog had lifted from his eyes he saw that he had signed his name.

"But . . ."

"Welcome to the Space Troopers," the sergeant boomed, smacking him on the back (trapezius like rock) and relieving him of the stylo. "FALL IN!" he called in a larger voice, and the recruits stumbled from the tavern.

"What have they done to my son!" Bill's mother screeched, coming into the market square, clutching at her bosom with one hand and towing his baby brother Charlie with the other. Charlie began to cry and wet his pants.

"Your son is now a trooper for the greater glory of the Emperor," the sergeant said, pushing his slack-jawed and round-shouldered recruit squad into line.

"No! it can't be . . ." Bill's mother sobbed, tearing at her graying hair. "I'm a poor widow, he's my sole support . . . you cannot . . . !"

"Mother . . ." Bill said, but the sergeant shoved him back into the ranks.

6

"Be brave, madam," he said. "There can be no greater glory for a mother." He dropped a large and newly minted coin into her hand. "Here is the enlistment bonus, the Emperor's shilling. I know he wants you to have it. ATTENTION!"

With a clash of heels the graceless recruits braced their shoulders and lifted their chins. Much to his surprise, so did Bill.

"RIGHT TURN!"

In a single, graceful motion they turned, as the command robot relayed the order to the hypno-coil in every boot. "FORWARD MARCH!" And they did, in perfect rhythm, so well under control that, try as hard as he could, Bill could neither turn his head nor wave a last good-by to his mother. She vanished behind him, and one last, anguished wail cut through the thud of marching feet.

"Step up the count to 130," the sergeant ordered, glancing at the watch set under the nail of his little finger. "Just ten miles to the station, and we'll be in camp tonight, my lads."

The command robot moved its metronome up one notch and the tramping boots conformed to the smarter pace and the men began to sweat. By the time they had reached the copter station it was nearly dark, their red paper uniforms hung in shreds, the gilt had been rubbed from their pot-metal buttons, and the surface charge that repelled the dust from their thin plastic boots had leaked away. They looked as ragged, weary, dusty, and miserable as they felt.

II

It wasn't the recorded bugle playing reveille that woke Bill but the supersonics that streamed through the metal frame of his bunk that shook him until the fillings vibrated from his teeth. He sprang to his feet and stood there shivering in the gray of dawn. Because it was summer the floor was refrigerated: no mollycoddling of the men in Camp Leon Trotsky. The pallid, chilled figures of the other recruits loomed up on every side, and when the soul-shaking vibrations had died away they dragged their thick sackcloth and sandpaper fatigue uniforms from their bunks, pulled them hastily on, jammed their feet into the great, purple recruit boots, and staggered out into the dawn.

"I am here to break your spirit," a voice rich with menace told them, and they looked up and shivered even more as they faced the chief demon in this particular hell.

Petty Chief Officer Deathwish Drang was a specialist from the tips of the angry spikes of his hair to the corrugated stamping-soles of his mirrorlike boots. He was wide-shouldered and lean-hipped, while his long arms hung, curved like those of some horrible anthropoid, the knuckles of his immense fists scarred from the breaking of thousands of teeth. It was impossible to look at this detestable form and imagine that it issued from the tender womb of a woman. He could never have been born; he must have been built to order by the government. Most terrible of all was the head. The face! The hairline was scarcely a finger's-width above the black tangle of the brows that were set like a rank growth of foliage at the rim of the black pits that concealed the eyes—visible only as baleful red gleams in the Stygian darkness. A nose, broken and crushed, squatted above the mouth that was like a knife slash in the taut belly of a corpse, while from between the lips issued the great, white fangs of the canine teeth, at least two inches long, that rested in grooves on the lower lip.

"I am Petty Chief Officer Deathwish Drang, and you will call me 'sir' or 'm'lord.'" He began to pace grimly before the row of terrified recruits. "I am your father and your mother and your whole universe and your dedicated enemy, and very soon I will have you regretting the day you were born. I will crush your will. When I say frog, you will jump. My job is to turn you into troopers, and troopers have discipline. Discipline means simply unthinking subservience, loss of free will, absolute obedience. That is all I ask . . ."

He stopped before Bill, who was not shaking quite as much as the others, and scowled.

"I don't like your face. One month of Sunday KP."

"Sir . . ."

"And a second month for talking back."

He waited, but Bill was silent. He had already learned his first lesson on how to be a good trooper. Keep your mouth shut. Deathwish paced on.

"Right now you are nothing but horrible, sordid, flabby pieces of debased civilian flesh. I shall turn that flesh to muscle, your wills to jelly, your minds to machines. You will become good troopers, or I will kill you. Very soon you will be hearing stories about me, vicious stories, about how I killed and ate a recruit who disobeyed me."

He halted and stared at them, and slowly the coffin-lid lips parted in an evil travesty of a grin, while a drop of saliva formed at the tip of each whitened tusk.

"That story is true."

A moan broke from the row of recruits, and they shook

as though a chill wind had passed over them. The smile vanished.

"We will run to breakfast now as soon as I have some volunteers for an easy assignment. Can any of you drive a helicar?"

Two recruits hopefully raised their hands, and he beckoned them forward. "All right, both of you, mops and buckets behind that door. Clean out the latrine while the rest are eating. You'll have a better appetite for lunch."

That was Bill's second lesson on how to be a good trooper: never volunteer.

The days of recruit training passed with a horribly lethargic speed. With each day conditions became worse and Bill's exhaustion greater. This seemed impossible, but it was nevertheless true. A large number of gifted and sadistic minds had designed it to be that way. The recruits' heads were shaved for uniformity. The food was theoretically nourishing but incredibly vile and when, by mistake, one batch of meat was served in an edible state it was caught at the last moment and thrown out and the cook reduced two grades. Their sleep was broken by mock gas attacks and their free time filled with caring for their equipment. The seventh day was designated as a day of rest, but they all had received punishments, like Bill's KP, and it was as any other day. On this, the third Sunday of their imprisonment, they were stumbling through the last hour of the day before the lights were extinguished and they were finally permitted to crawl into their casehardened bunks. Bill pushed against the weak force field that blocked the door, cunningly designed to allow the desert flies to enter but not leave the barracks, and dragged himself in. After fourteen hours of KP his legs vibrated with exhaustion, and his arms were wrinkled and pallid as a corpse's from the soapy water. He dropped his jacket to the floor, where it stood stiffly supported by its burden of sweat, grease, and dust, and dragged his shaver from his footlocker. In the latrine he bobbed his head around trying to find a clear space on one of the mirrors. All of them had been heavily stenciled in large letters with such inspiring messages as KEEP YOUR WUG SHUT—THE CHINGERS ARE LISTENING and IF YOU TALK THIS MAN MAY DIE. He finally plugged the shaver in next to WOULD YOU WANT YOUR SISTER TO MARRY ONE? and centered his face in the O in ONE. Black-rimmed and blood-shot eyes stared back at him as he ran the buzzing machine over the underweight planes of his jaw. It took more than a minute for the meaning of the question to penetrate his fatigue-drugged brain.

"I haven't got a sister," he grumbled peevishly, "and if I did, why should she want to marry a lizard anyway?" It was a rhetorical question, but it brought an answer from the far end of the room, from the last shot tower in the second row.

"It doesn't mean *exactly* what it says—it's just there to make us hate the dirty enemy more."

Bill jumped, he had thought he was alone in the latrine, and the razor buzzed spitefully and gouged a bit of flesh from his lip.

"Who's there? Why are you hiding?" he snarled, then recognized the huddled dark figure and the many pairs of boots. "Oh, it's only you, Eager." His anger drained away, and he turned back to the mirror.

Eager Beager was so much a part of the latrine that you forgot he was there. A moon-faced, eternally smiling youth, whose apple-red cheeks never lost their glow and whose smile looked so much out of place here in Camp Leon Trotsky that everyone wanted to kill him until they remembered that he was mad. He had to be mad because he was always eager to help his buddies and had volunteered as permanent latrine orderly. Not only that, but he liked to polish boots and had offered to do those of one after another of his buddies until now he did the boots for every man in the squad every night. Whenever they were in the barracks Eager Beager could be found crouched at the end of the thrones that were his personal domain, surrounded by the heaps of shoes and polishing industriously, his face wreathed in smiles. He would still be there after lights-out, working by the light of a burning wick stuck in a can of polish, and was usually up before the others in the morning, finishing his voluntary job and still smiling. Sometimes, when the boots were very dirty, he worked right through the night. The kid was obviously insane, but no one turned him in because he did such a good job on the boots, and they all prayed that he wouldn't die of exhaustion until recruit training was finished.

"Well if that's what they want to say, why don't they just say, 'Hate the dirty enemy more,'" Bill complained. He jerked his thumb at the far wall, where there was a poster labeled KNOW THE ENEMY. It featured a life-sized illustration of a Chinger, a seven-foot-high saurian that looked very much like a scale-covered, four-armed, green kangaroo with an alligator's head. "Whose sister would want to marry a thing like that anyway? And what would a thing like that want to do with a sister, except maybe eat her?"

Eager put a last buff on a purple toe and picked up another boot. He frowned for a brief instant to show what a serious thought this was. "Well you see, gee—it doesn't mean a *real* sister. It's just part of psychological warfare. We have to win the war. To win the war we have to fight hard. In order to fight hard we have to have good soldiers. Good soldiers have to hate the enemy. That's the way it goes. The Chingers are the only non-human race that has been discovered in the galaxy that has gone beyond the aboriginal level, so naturally we have to wipe them out."

"What the hell do you mean, *naturally?* I don't want to

wipe anyone out. I just want to go home and be a Technical Fertilizer Operator."

"Well, I don't mean you personally, of course—gee!" Eager opened a fresh can of polish with purple-stained hands and dug his fingers into it. "I mean the human race, that's just the way we do things. If we don't wipe them out they'll wipe us out. Of course they say that war is against their religion and they will only fight in defense, and they have never made any attacks yet. But we can't believe them, even though it is true. They might change their religion or their minds some day, and then where would we be? The best answer is to wipe them out now."

Bill unplugged his razor and washed his face in the tepid, rusty water. "It still doesn't seem to make sense. All right, so the sister I don't have doesn't marry one of them. But how about that—" he pointed to the stenciling on the duckboards, KEEP THIS SHOWER CLEAR—THE ENEMY CAN HEAR. "Or that—" The sign above the urinal that read BUTTON FLIES—BEWARE SPIES. "Forgetting for the moment that we don't have any secrets here worth traveling a mile to hear, much less twenty-five light years—how could a Chinger possibly be a spy? What kind of make-up would disguise a seven-foot lizard as a recruit? You couldn't even disguise one to look like Deathwish Drang, though you could get pretty close—"

The lights went out, and, as though using his name had summoned him like a devil from the pit, the voice of Deathwish blasted through the barracks.

"Into your sacks! Into your sacks! Don't you lousy bowbs know there's a war on!"

Bill stumbled away through the darkness of the barracks where the only illumination was the red glow from Deathwish's eyes. He fell asleep the instant his head touched his carborundum pillow, and it seemed that only a moment had elapsed before reveille sent him hurtling from his bunk. At breakfast, while he was painfully cutting his coffee-substitute into chunks small enough to swallow, the telenews reported heavy fighting in the Beta Lyra sector with mounting losses. A groan rippled through the mess hall when this was announced, not because of any excess of patriotism but because any bad news would only make things worse for them. They did not know how this would be arranged, but they were positive it would be. They were right. Since the morning was a bit cooler than usual the Monday parade was postponed until noon when the ferro-concrete drill ground would have warmed up nicely and there would be the maximum number of heat-prostration cases. But this was just the beginning. From where Bill stood at attention near the rear he could see that the air-conditioned canopy was up on the reviewing stand. That meant brass. The trigger guard of his atomic rifle dug a hole into his shoulder, and a drop of sweat collected, then dripped from the tip of his nose. Out of the corners of his eyes he could see the steady ripple of motion as men collapsed here and there among the massed ranks of thousands and were dragged to the waiting ambulances by alert corpsmen. Here they were laid in the shade of the vehicles until they revived and could be urged back to their positions in the formation.

Then the band burst into "Spacemen Ho and Chingers Vanquished!" and the broadcast signal to each boot heel snapped the ranks to attention at the same instant, and the thousands of rifles flashed in the sun. The commanding general's staff car—this was obvious from the two stars painted on it—pulled up beside the reviewing stand and a tiny, round figure moved quickly through the furnacelike air to the comfort of the enclosure. Bill had never seen him any closer than this, at least from the front, though once while he was returning from late KP he had spotted the general getting into his car near the camp theater. At least Bill thought it was he, but all he had seen was a brief rear view. Therefore, if he had a mental picture of the general, it was of a large backside superimposed on a teeny, antlike figure. He thought of most officers in these general terms, since the men of course had nothing to do with officers during their recruit training. Bill had had a good glimpse of a second lieutenant once, near the orderly room, and he knew he had a face. And there had been a medical officer no more than thirty yards away, who had lectured them on venereal disease, but Bill had been lucky enough to sit behind a post and had promptly fallen asleep.

After the band shut up the anti-G loudspeakers floated out over the troops, and the general addressed them. He had nothing to say that anyone cared to listen to, and he closed with the announcement that because of losses in the field their training program would be accelerated, which is just what they had expected. Then the band played some more and they marched back to the barracks, changed into their haircloth fatigues, and marched—double time now—to the range, where they fired their atomic rifles at plastic replicas of Chingers that popped up out of holes in the ground. Their aim was bad until Deathwish Drang popped out of a hole and every trooper switched to full automatic and hit with every charge fired from every gun, which is a very hard thing to do. Then the smoke cleared, and they stopped cheering and started sobbing when they saw that it was only a plastic replica of Deathwish, now torn to tiny pieces, and the original appeared behind them and gnashed its tusks and gave them all a full month's KP.

"The human body is a wonderful thing," Bowb Brown said a month later, when they were sitting around a table in the Lowest Ranks Klub eating plastic-skinned sausages stuffed with road sweepings and drinking watery warm beer. Bowb

Brown was a thoat-herder from the plains, which is why they called him Bowb, since everyone knows just what thoat-herders do with their thoats. He was tall, thin, and bow-legged, his skin burnt to the color of ancient leather. He rarely talked, being more used to the eternal silence of the plains broken only by the eerie cry of the restless thoat, but he was a great thinker, since the one thing he had plenty of was time to think in. He could worry a thought for days, even weeks, before he mentioned it aloud, and while he was thinking about it nothing could disturb him. He even let them call him Bowb without protesting: call any other trooper bowb and he would hit you in the face. Bill and Eager and the other troopers from X squad sitting around the table all clapped and cheered, as they always did when Bowb said something.

"Tell us more, Bowb!"

"It can still talk—I thought it was dead!"

"Go on—why is the body a wonderful thing?"

They waited in expectant silence, while Bowb managed to tear a bite from his sausage and, after ineffectual chewing, swallowed it with an effort that brought tears to his eyes. He eased the pain with a mouthful of beer and spoke.

"The human body is a wonderful thing, because if it doesn't die it lives."

They waited for more until they realized that he was finished, then they sneered.

"Boy, are you full of bowb!"

"Sign up for OCS!"

"Yeah—but what does it *mean?*"

Bill knew what it meant but didn't tell them. There were only half as many men in the squad as there had been the first day. One man had been transferred, but all the others were in the hospital, or in the mental hospital, or discharged for the convenience of the government as being too crippled for active service. Or dead. The survivors, after losing every ounce of weight not made up of bone or essential connective tissue, had put back the lost weight in the form of muscle and were now completely adapted to the rigors of Camp Leon Trotsky, though they still loathed it. Bill marveled at the efficiency of the system. Civilians had to fool around with examinations, grades, retirement benefits, seniority, and a thousand other factors that limited the efficiency of the workers. But how easily the troopers did it! They simply killed off the weaker ones and used the survivors. He respected the system. Though he still loathed it.

"You know what I need, I need a woman," Ugly Uggles-way said.

"Don't talk dirty," Bill told him promptly, since he had been correctly brought up.

"I'm not talking dirty!" Ugly whined. "It's not like I said I wanted to re-enlist or that I thought Deathwish was human or anything like that. I just said I need a woman. Don't we all?"

"I need a drink," Bowb Brown said as he took a long swig from his glass of dehydrated reconstituted beer, shuddered, then squirted it out through his teeth in a long stream onto the concrete, where it instantly evaporated.

"Affirm, affirm," Ugly agreed, bobbing his mat-haired, warty head up and down. "I need a woman *and* a drink." His whine became almost plaintive. "After all, what else is there to want in the troopers outside of out?"

They thought about that a long time, but could think of nothing else that anyone really wanted. Eager Beager looked out from under the table, where he was surreptitiously polishing a boot and said that he wanted more polish, but they ignored him. Even Bill, now that he put his mind to it, could think of nothing he really wanted other than this inextricably linked pair. He tried hard to think of something else, since he had vague memories of wanting other things when he had been a civilian, but nothing else came to mind.

"Gee, it's only seven weeks more until we get our first pass," Eager said from under the table, then screamed a little as everyone kicked him at once.

But slow as subjective time crawled by, the objective clocks were still operating, and the seven weeks did pass by and eliminate themselves one by one. Busy weeks filled with all the essential recruit-training courses: bayonet drill, small-arms training, short-arm inspection, greypfing, orientation lectures, drill, communal singing and the Articles of War. These last were read with dreadful regularity twice a week and were absolute torture because of the intense somnolence they brought on. At the first rustle of the scratchy, monotonous voice from the tape player heads would begin to nod. But every seat in the auditorium was wired with an EEG that monitored the brain waves of the captive troopers. As soon as the shape of the Alpha wave indicated transition from consciousness to slumber a powerful jolt of current would be shot into the dozing buttocks, jabbing the owners painfully awake. The musty auditorium was a dimly lit torture chamber, filled with the droning, dull voice, punctuated by the sharp screams of the electrified, the sea of nodding heads abob here and there with painfully leaping figures.

No one ever listened to the terrible executions and sentences announced in the Articles for the most innocent of crimes. Everyone knew that they had signed away all human rights when they enlisted, and the itemizing of what they had lost interested them not in the slightest. What they really were interested in was counting the hours until they would receive their first pass. The ritual by which this reward was begrudgingly given was unusually humiliating, but they expected this and merely lowered their eyes and shuffled forward in the line, ready to sacrifice any remaining shards of their self-respect in exchange for the crimpled scrap of plastic. This rite finished, there was a scramble for the monorail train whose track ran on electrically charged pillars, soaring over the thirty-foot-high barbed wire, crossing the quicksand beds, then dropping into the little farming town of Leyville.

At least it had been an agricultural town before Camp Leon Trotsky had been built, and sporadically, in the hours when the troopers weren't on leave, it followed its original agrarian bent. The rest of the time the grain and feed stores shut down and the drink and knocking shops opened. Many times the same premises were used for both functions. A lever would be pulled when the first of the leave party thundered out of the station and grain bins became beds, salesclerks pimps, cashiers retained their same function—though the prices went up—while counters would be racked with glasses to serve as bars. It was to one of these establishments, a mortuary-cum-saloon, that Bill and his friends went.

"What'll it be, boys?" the ever smiling owner of the Final Resting Bar and Grill asked.

"Double shot of Embalming Fluid," Bowb Brown told him.

"No jokes," the landlord said, the smile vanishing for a second as he took down a bottle on which the garish label REAL WHISKEY had been pasted over the etched-in EMBALMING FLUID. "Any trouble I call the MPs." The smile returned as money struck the counter. "Name your poison, gents."

They sat around a long, narrow table as thick as it was wide, with brass handles on both sides, and let the blessed relief of ethyl alcohol trickle a path down their dust-lined throats.

"I never drank before I came into the service," Bill said, draining four fingers neat of Old Kidney Killer and held his glass out for more.

"You never had to," Ugly said, pouring.

"That's for sure," Bowb Brown said, smacking his lips with relish and raising a bottle to his lips again.

"Gee," Eager Beager said, sipping hesitantly at the edge of his glass, "it tastes like a tincture of sugar, wood chips, various esters, and a number of higher alcohols."

"Drink up," Bowb said incoherently around the neck of the bottle. "All them things is good for you."

"Now I want a woman," Ugly said, and there was a rush as they all jammed in the door, trying to get out at the same time, until someone shouted, "Look!" and they turned to see Eager still sitting at the table.

"Woman!" Ugly said enthusiastically, in the tone of voice you say Dinner! when you are calling a dog. The knot of men stirred in the doorway and stamped their feet. Eager didn't move.

"Gee—I think I'll stay right here," he said, his smile simpler than ever. "But you guys run along."

"Don't you feel well, Eager?"

"Feel fine."

"Ain't you reached puberty?"

"Gee . . ."

"What you gonna do here?"

Eager reached under the table and dragged out a canvas grip. He opened it to show them that it was packed with great purple boots. "I thought I'd catch up on my polishing."

They walked slowly down the wooden sidewalk, silent for the moment. "I wonder if there is something wrong with Eager?" Bill asked, but no one answered him. They were looking down the rutted street, at a brilliantly illuminated sign that cast a tempting, ruddy glow.

SPACEMEN'S REST it said. CONTINUOUS STRIP SHOW and BEST DRINKS and better PRIVATE ROOMS FOR GUESTS AND THEIR FRIENDS. They walked faster. The front wall of the Spacemen's Rest was covered with shatterproof glass cases filled with tri-di pix of the fully dressed (bangle and double stars) entertainers, and further in with pix of them nude (debangled with fallen stars). Bill stayed the quick sound of panting by pointing to a small sign almost lost among the tumescent wealth of mammaries.

OFFICERS ONLY it read.

"Move along," an MP grated, and poked at them with his electronic nightstick. They shuffled on.

The next establishment admitted men of all classes, but the cover charge was seventy-seven credits, more than they all had between them. After that the OFFICERS ONLY began again, until the pavement ended and all the lights were behind them.

"What's that?" Ugly asked at the sound of murmured voices from a nearby darkened street, and peering closely they saw a line of troopers that stretched out of sight around a distant corner. "What's this?" he asked the last man in the line.

"Lower-ranks cathouse. Two credits, two minutes. And don't try to buck the line, bowb. On the back, on the back."

They joined up instantly, and Bill ended up last, but not for long. They shuffled forward slowly, and other troopers appeared and cued up behind him. The night was cool, and he took many life-preserving slugs from his bottle. There was little conversation and what there was died as the red-lit portal loomed ever closer. It opened and closed at regular intervals, and one by one Bill's buddies slipped in to partake of its satisfying, though rapid, pleasures. Then it was his turn and the door started to open and he started to step forward and the sirens started to scream and a large MP with a great fat belly jumped between Bill and the door.

"Emergency recall. Back to the base you men!" it barked.

Bill howled a strangled groan of frustration and leaped forward, but a light tap with the electronic nightstick sent him reeling back with the others. He was carried along, half stunned, with the shuffling wave of bodies, while the sirens moaned and the artificial northern lights in the sky spelled out To Arms!!!! in letters of flame each a hundred miles long. Someone put his hand out, holding Bill up as he started to slide under the trampling purple boots. It was his old buddy, Ugly, carrying a satiated smirk and he hated him and tried to hit him. But before he could raise his fist they were swept into a monorail car, hurtled through the night, and disgorged back in Camp Leon Trotsky. He forgot his anger when the gnarled claws of Deathwish Drang dragged them from the crowd.

"Pack your bags," he rasped. "You're shipping out."

"They can't do that to us—we haven't finished our training."

"They can do whatever they want, and they usually do. A glorious space battle has just been fought to its victorious conclusion and there are over four million casualties, give or take a hundred thousand. Replacements are needed, which is you. Prepare to board the transports immediately if not sooner."

"We can't—we have no space gear! The supply room . . ."

"All of the supply personnel have already been shipped out."

"Food . . ."

"The cooks and KP pushers are already spacebound. This is an emergency. All non-essential personnel are being sent out. Probably to die." He twanged a tusk coyly and washed them with his loathsome grin. "While I remain here in peaceful security to train your replacements." The delivery tube plunked at his elbow, and as he opened the message capsule and read its contents his smile slowly fell to pieces. "They're shipping me out too," he said hollowly.

III

A total of 89,672,899 recruits had already been shipped into space through Camp Leon Trotsky, so the process was an automatic and smoothly working one, even though this time it was processing itself, like a snake swallowing its own tail. Bill and his buddies were the last group of recruits through, and the snake began ingesting itself right behind them. No sooner had they been shorn of their sprouting fuzz and deloused in the ultrasonic delouser than the barbers rushed at each other and in a welter of under and over arms, gobbets of hair, shards of mustache, bits of flesh, drops of blood, they clipped and shaved each other, then pulled the operator after them into the ultrasonic chamber. Medical corpsmen gave themselves injections against rocket-fever and space-cafard; record clerks issued themselves pay books; and the loadmasters kicked each other up the ramps and into the waiting shuttleships. Rockets blasted, living columns of fire like scarlet tongues licking down at the blasting pads, burning up the ramps in a lovely pyrotechnic display, since the ramp operators were also aboard. The ships echoed and thundered up into the night sky leaving Camp Leon Trotsky a dark and silent ghost town where bits of daily orders and punishment rosters rustled and blew from the bulletin boards, dancing through the deserted streets to finally plaster themselves against the noisy, bright windows of the Officers' Club where a great drinking party was in progress, although there was much complaining because the officers had to serve themselves.

Up and up the shuttleships shot, toward the great fleet of

deep-spacers that darkened the stars above, a new fleet, the most powerful the galaxy had ever seen, so new in fact that the ships were still under construction. Welding torches flared in brilliant points of light while hot rivets hurled their flat trajectories across the sky into the waiting buckets. The spots of light died away as one behemoth of the star lanes was completed and thin screams sounded in the space-suit radio circuit as the workers, instead of being returned to the yards, were pressed into service on the ship they had so recently built. This was total war.

Bill staggered through the sagging plastic tube that connected the shuttleship to a dreadnaught of space and dropped his bags in front of a petty chief officer who sat at a desk in the hangar-sized spacelock. Or rather he tried to drop it, but since there was no gravity the bags remained in mid-air, and when he pushed them down he rose (since a body when it is falling freely is said to be in free fall, and anything with weight has no weight, and for every action there is an equal and opposite reaction or something like that). The petty looked up and snarled and pulled Bill back down to the deck.

"None of your bowby spacelubber tricks, trooper. Name?"

"Bill, spelled with two L's."

"Bil," the petty mumbled, licking the end of his stylo, then inscribing it in the ship's roster with round, illiterate letters. "Two 'L's' for officers only, bowb—learn your place. What's your classification?"

"Recruit, unskilled, untrained, spacesick."

"Well don't puke in here, that's what you have your own quarters for. You are now a Fuse Tender Sixth Class, unskilled. Bunk down in compartment 34J-89T-001. Move. And keep that woopsy-sack over your head."

No sooner had Bill found his quarters and thrown his bags into a bunk, where they floated five inches over the reclaimed rock-wool mattress, than Eager Beager came in, followed by

24

Bowb Brown and a crowd of strangers, some of them carrying welding torches and angry expressions.

"Where's Ugly and the rest of the squad?" Bill asked.

Bowb shrugged and strapped himself into his bunk for a little shut-eye. Eager opened one of the six bags he always carried and removed some boots to polish.

"Are you saved?" A deep voice, vibrant with emotion, sounded from the other end of the compartment. Bill looked up, startled, and the big trooper standing there saw the motion and stabbed toward him with an immense finger. "You, brother, are you saved?"

"That's a little hard to say," Bill mumbled, bending over and rooting in his bag, hoping the man would go away. But he didn't; in fact, he came over and sat down on Bill's bunk. Bill tried to ignore him, but this was hard to do, because the trooper was over six feet high, heavily muscled, and iron-jawed. He had lovely, purplish-black skin that made Bill a little jealous, because his was only a sort of grayish pink. Since the trooper's shipboard uniform was almost the same shade of black, he looked all of a piece, very effective with his flashing smile and piercing gaze.

"Welcome aboard the *Christine Keeler*," he said, and with a friendly shake splintered most of Bill's knucklebones. "The grand old lady of this fleet, commissioned almost a week ago. I'm the Reverend Fuse Tender Sixth Class Tembo, and I see by the stencil on your bag that your name is Bill, and since we're shipmates, Bill, please call me Tembo, and how is the condition of your soul?"

"I haven't had much chance to think about it lately . . ."

"I should think not, just coming from recruit training, since attendance of chapel during training is a court-martial offense. But that's all behind you now and you can be saved. Might I ask if you are of the faith . . . ?"

"My folks were Fundamentalist Zoroastrian, so I suppose . . ."

"Superstition, my boy, rank superstition. It was the hand of fate that brought us together in this ship, that your soul would have this one chance to be saved from the fiery pit. You've heard of Earth?"

"I like plain food . . ."

"It's a planet, my boy—the home of the human race. The home from whence we all sprang, see it, a green and lovely world, a jewel in space." Tembo had slipped a tiny projector from his pocket while he spoke, and a colored image appeared on the bulkhead, a planet swimming artistically through the void, girdled by white clouds. Suddenly ruddy lightning shot through the clouds, and they twisted and boiled while great wounds appeared on the planet below. From the pinhead speaker came the tiny sound of rolling thunder. "But wars sprang up among the sons of man and they smote each other with the atomic energies until the Earth itself groaned aloud and mighty was the holocaust. And when the final lightnings stilled there was death in the North, death in the West, death in the East, death, death, death. Do you realize what that means?" Tembo's voice was eloquent with feeling, suspended for an instant in mid-flight, waiting for the answer to the catechistical question.

"I'm not quite sure," Bill said, rooting aimlessly in his bag, "I come from Phigerinadon II, it's a quieter place . . ."

"There was no death in the SOUTH! And why was the South spared, I ask you, and the answer is because it was the will of Samedi that all the false prophets and false religions and false gods be wiped from the face of the Earth so that the only true faith should remain. The First Reformed Voodoo Church . . ."

General Quarters sounded, a hooting alarm keyed to the resonant frequency of the human skull so that the bone vibrated as though the head were inside a mighty bell, and the eyes blurred out of focus with each stroke. There was a scramble for the passageway, where the hideous sound was not quite as loud and where non-coms were waiting to herd them to their stations. Bill followed Eager Beager up an oily ladder and out of the hatch in the floor of the fuse room. Great racks of fuses stretched away on all sides of them, while from the tops of the racks sprang arm-thick cables that looped upward and vanished through the ceiling. In front of the racks, evenly spaced, were round openings a foot in diameter.

"My opening remarks will be brief, any trouble from any of you and I will personally myself feed you head first down the nearest fuseway." A greasy forefinger pointed at one of the holes in the deck, and they recognized the voice of their new master. He was shorter and wider and thicker in the gut than Deathwish, but there was a generic resemblance that was unmistakable. "I am Fuse Tender First Class Spleen. I will take you crumbly, ground-crawling bowbs and will turn you into highly skilled and efficient fuse tenders or else feed you down the nearest fuseway. This is a highly skilled and efficient technical speciality which usually takes a year to train a good man but this is war so you are going to learn to do it now or else. I will now demonstrate. Tembo front and center. Take board 19J-9, it's out of circuit now."

Tembo clashed his heels and stood at rigid attention in front of the board. Stretching away on both sides of him were the fuses, white ceramic cylinders capped on both ends with metal, each one a foot in diameter, five feet high, and weighing ninety pounds. There was a red band around the midriff of each fuse. First Class Spleen tapped one of these bands.

"Every fuse has one of these red bands, which is called a fuseband and is of the color red. When the fuse burns out this band turns black. I don't expect you to remember all this now, but it's in your manual and you are going to be

27

letter-perfect before I am done with you, or else. Now I will show you what will happen when a fuse burns out. Tembo— that is a burned-out fuse! Go!"

"Unggh!" Tembo shouted, and leaped at the fuse and grasped it with both hands. "Unggh!" he said again, as he pulled it from the clips, and again "Unggh!" when he dropped it into the fuseway. Then, still Ungghing, he pulled a new fuse from the storage rack and clipped it into place and with a final Unggh! snapped back to attention.

"And that's the way it is done, by the count, by the numbers, the trooper way, and you are going to learn it or else." A dull buzzing sounded, grumbling through the air like a stifled eructation. "There's the chow call, so I'll let you break now, and while you're eating, think about what you are going to have to learn. Fall out."

Other troopers were going by in the corridor, and they followed them into the bowels of the ship.

"Gee—do you think the food might be any better than it was back in camp?" Eager asked, smacking his lips excitedly.

"It is completely impossible that it could be any worse," Bill said as they joined a line leading to a door labeled Con-solidated Mess Number Two. "Any change will have to make it better. After all—aren't we fighting troopers now? We have to go into combat fit, the manual says."

The line moved forward with painful slowness, but within an hour they were at the door. Inside the room a tired-looking KP in soap-stained, greasy fatigues handed Bill a yellow plastic cup from a rack before him. Bill moved on, and when the trooper in front of him stepped away, he faced a blank wall from which there emerged a single, handleless spigot. A fat cook standing next to it, wearing a large white chef's hat and a soiled undershirt, waved him forward with the soup ladle in his hand.

"C'mon, c'mon, ain't you never et before? Cup under the spout, dog tag in the slot, snap it up!"

Bill held the cup as he had been advised and noticed a narrow slit in the metal wall just at eye level. His dog tags were hanging around his neck, and he pushed one of them into the slot. Something went *bzzzzz*, and a thin stream of yellow fluid gushed out, filling the cup halfway.

"Next man!" the cook shouted, and pulled Bill away so that Eager could take his place. "What is this?" Bill asked, peering into the cup.

"What is this! What is this!" the cook raged, growing bright red. "This is your dinner, you stupid bowb! This is absolutely chemically pure water in which are dissolved eighteen amino acids, sixteen vitamins, eleven mineral salts, a fatty acid ester, and glucose. What else did you expect?"

"Dinner . . . ?" Bill said hopefully, then saw red as the soup ladle crashed down on his head. "Could I have it without the fatty acid ester?" he asked hopefully, but he was pushed out into the corridor where Eager joined him.

"Gee," Eager said. "This has all the food elements necessary to sustain life indefinitely. Isn't that marvelous?"

Bill sipped at his cup, then sighed tremulously.

"Look at that," Tembo said, and when Bill turned, a projected image appeared on the corridor wall. It showed a misty firmament, in which tiny figures seemed to be riding on clouds. "Hell awaits you, my boy, unless you are saved. Turn your back on your superstitious ways, for the First Reformed Voodoo Church welcomes you with open arms; come unto her bosom, and find your place in heaven at Samedi's right hand. Sit there with Mondongue and Bakalou and Zandor, who will welcome you."

The projected scene changed; the clouds grew closer, while from the little speaker came the tiny sound of a heavenly choir with drum accompaniment. Now the figures could be seen clearly, all with very dark skins and white robes from the back of which protruded great black wings. They smiled and waved gracefully to each other as their clouds passed, while singing enthusiastically and beating on the little tom-toms that each one carried. It was a lovely scene, and Bill's eyes misted a bit.

"Attention!"

The barking tones echoed from the walls and the troopers snapped their shoulders back, heels together, eyes ahead. The heavenly choir vanished as Tembo shoved the projector back into his pocket.

"As you was," First Class Spleen ordered, and they turned to see him leading two MPs with drawn handguns who were acting as bodyguards for an officer. Bill knew it was an officer because they had had an officer-identification course, plus the fact that there was a KNOW YOUR OFFICERS chart on the latrine wall that he had had a great deal of opportunity to study during an anguilluliasis epidemic. His jaw gaped open as the officer went by, almost close enough to *touch,* and stopped in front of Tembo.

"Fuse Tender Sixth Class Tembo, I have good news for you. In two weeks your seven-year period of enlistment will be up, and because of your fine record Captain Zekial has authorized a doubling of the usual mustering-out pay, an honorable discharge with band music, as well as your free transport back to Earth."

Tembo, relaxed and firm, looked down at the runty lieuten-ant with the well-chewed blond mustache who stood before him. "That will be impossible, sir."

"Impossible!" the lieutenant screeched, and rocked back and forth on his high-heeled boots. "Who are *you* to tell *me* what is impossible . . . !"

"Not I, sir," Tembo answered with utmost calm. "Regula-tion 13-9A, paragraph 45, page 8923, volume 43 of Rules,

Regulations and Articles of War. 'No man nor officer shall or will receive a discharge other than dishonorable with death sentence from a vessel, post, base, camp, ship, outpost, or labor camp during time of emergency . . .'"

"Are you a ship's lawyer, Tembo?"

"No, sir. I'm a loyal trooper, sir. I just want to do my duty, sir."

"There's something very funny about you, Tembo. I saw in your record that you enlisted *voluntarily* without drugs and or hypnotics being used. Now you refuse discharge. That's bad, Tembo, very bad. Gives you a bad name. Makes you look suspicious. Makes you look like a spy or something."

"I'm a loyal trooper, of the Emperor, sir, not a spy."

"You're not a spy, Tembo, we have looked into that very carefully. But why *are* you in the service, Tembo?"

"To be a loyal trooper of the Emperor, sir, and to do my best to spread the gospel. Have you been saved, sir?"

"Watch your tongue, trooper or I'll have you up on charges! Yes, we know that story—*Reverend*—but we don't believe it. You're being too tricky, but we'll find out . . ." He stalked away, muttering to himself, and they all snapped to attention until he was gone. The other troopers looked at Tembo oddly and did not feel comfortable until he had gone. Bill and Eager walked slowly back to their quarters.

"Turned down a discharge . . . !" Bill mumbled in awe.

"Gee," Eager said, "maybe he's nuts. I can't think of any other reason."

"Nobody could be *that* crazy," Bill said. "I wonder what's in there?" pointing to a door with a large sign that read Admittance to Authorized Personnel Only.

"Gee—I don't know—maybe food?"

They slipped through instantly and closed the door behind them, but there was no food there. Instead they were in a long chamber with one curved wall, while attached to this

31

wall were cumbersome devices each set with meters, dials, switches, controls, levers, a view screen, and a relief tube. Bill bent over and read the label on the nearest one.

"*Mark IV Atomic Blaster*—and look at the size of them! This must be the ship's main battery." He turned around and saw that Eager was holding his arm up so that his wrist watch pointed at the guns and was pressing on the crown with the index finger of his other hand.

"What are you doing?" Bill asked.

"Gee—just seeing what time it was."

"How can you tell what time it is when you have the inside of your wrist toward your face and the watch is on the outside?"

Footsteps echoed far down the long gun deck, and they remembered the sign on the outside of the door. In an instant they had slipped back through it, and Bill pressed it quietly shut. When he turned around Eager Beager had gone so that he had to make his way back to their quarters by himself. Eager had returned first and was busy shining boots for his buddies and didn't look up when Bill came in.

But what *had* he been doing with his watch?

IV

This question kept bugging Bill all the time during the days of their training as they painfully learned the drill of fuse tending. It was an exacting, technical job that demanded all their attention, but in spare moments Bill worried. He worried when they stood in line for chow, and he worried during the few moments every night between the time the lights were turned off and sleep descended heavily upon his fatigue-drugged body. He worried whenever he had the time to do it, and he lost weight.

He lost weight not because he was worrying, but for the same reason everyone else lost weight. The shipboard rations. They were designed to sustain life, and that they did, but no mention was made of what kind of life it was to be. It was a dreary, underweight, hungry one. Yet Bill took no notice of this. He had a bigger problem, and he needed help. After Sunday drill at the end of their second week, he stayed to talk to First Class Spleen instead of joining the others in their tottering run toward the mess hall.

"I have a problem, sir . . ."

"You ain't the only one, but one shot cures it and you ain't a man until you've had it."

"It's not that kind of a problem. I'd like to . . . see the . . . chaplain . . ."

Spleen turned white and sank back against the bulkhead. "Now I heard everything," he said weakly. "Get down to chow, and if you don't tell anyone about this I won't either."

Bill blushed. "I'm sorry about this, First Class Spleen, but I can't help it. It's not my fault I have to see him, it could have happened to anyone . . ." His voice trailed away, and he looked down at his feet, rubbing one boot against another. The silence stretched out until Spleen finally spoke, but all the comradeliness was gone from his voice.

"All right, trooper—if that's the way you want it. But I hope none of the rest of the boys hear about it. Skip chow and get up there now—here's a pass." He scrawled on a scrap of paper then threw it contemptuously to the floor, turning and walking away as Bill bent humbly to pick it up.

Bill went down dropchutes, along corridors, through passageways, and up ladders. In the ship's directory the chaplain was listed as being in compartment 362-B on the 89th deck, and Bill finally found this, a plain metal door set with rivets. He raised his hand to knock, while sweat stood out in great beads from his face and his throat was dry. His knuckles boomed hollowly on the panel, and after an endless period a muffled voice sounded from the other side.

"Yeah, yeah—c'mon in—it's open."

Bill stepped through and snapped to attention when he saw the officer behind the single desk that almost filled the tiny room. The officer, a fourth lieutenant, though still young was balding rapidly. There were black circles under his eyes, and he needed a shave. His tie was knotted crookedly and badly crumpled. He continued to scratch among the stacks of paper that littered the desk, picking them up, changing piles with them, scrawling notes on some and throwing others into an overflowing wastebasket. When he moved one of the stacks Bill saw a sign on the desk that read LAUNDRY OFFICER.

"Excuse me, sir," he said, "but I am in the wrong office. I was looking for the chaplain."

"This is the chaplain's office but he's not on duty until 1300 hours, which is, as someone even as stupid-looking as you can tell, is in fifteen minutes more."

"Thank you, sir, I'll come back . . ." Bill slid toward the door.

"You'll stay and work." The officer raised bloodshot eyeballs and cackled evilly. "I got you. You can sort the hanky reports. I've lost six hundred jockstraps, and they may be in there. You think it's easy to be a laundry officer?" He sniveled with self-pity and pushed a tottering stack of papers over to Bill, who began to sort through them. Long before he was finished the buzzer sounded that ended the watch.

"I knew it!" the officer sobbed hopelessly, "this job will never end; instead it gets worse and worse. And you think *you* got problems!" He reached out an unsteady finger and flipped the sign on his desk over. It read CHAPLAIN on the other side. Then he grabbed the end of his necktie and pulled it back hard over his right shoulder. The necktie was fastened to his collar and the collar was set into ball bearings that rolled smoothly in a track fixed to his shirt. There was a slight whirring sound as the collar rotated; then the necktie was hanging out of sight down his back and his collar was now on backward, showing white and smooth and cool to the front.

The chaplain steepled his fingers before him, lowered his eyes, and smiled sweetly. "How may I help you, my son?"

"I thought you were the laundry officer," Bill said, taken aback.

"I am, my son, but that is just one of the burdens that must fall upon my shoulders. There is little call for a chaplain in these troubled times, but much call for a laundry officer. I do my best to serve." He bent his head humbly.

"But—which are you? A chaplain who is a part-time laundry officer, or a laundry officer who is a part-time chaplain?"

"That is a mystery, my son. There are some things that it

35

is best not to know. But I see you are troubled. May I ask if you are of the faith?"

"Which faith?"

"That's what I'm asking *you!*" the chaplain snapped, and for a moment the Old Laundry Officer peeped through. "How can I help you if I do not know what your religion is?"

"Fundamentalist Zoroastrian."

The chaplain took a plastic-covered sheet from a drawer and ran his finger down it. "Z . . . Z . . . Zen . . . Zodomite . . . Zoroastrian, Reformed Fundamentalist, is that the one?"

"Yes, sir."

"Well, should be no trouble with this, my son . . . 21–52–05 . . . ." He quickly dialed the number on a control plate set into the desk; then, with a grand gesture and an evangelistic gleam in his eye, he swept all the laundry papers to the floor. Hidden machinery hummed briefly, a portion of the desk top dropped away and reappeared a moment later bearing a black plastic box decorated with golden bulls, rampant. "Be with you in a second," the chaplain said, opening the box.

First he unrolled a length of white cloth sewn with more golden bulls and draped this around his neck. He placed a thick, leather-bound book next to the box, then on the closed lid set two metal bulls with hollowed-out backs. Into one of them he poured distilled water from a plastic flask and into the other sweet oil, which he ignited. Bill watched these familiar arrangements with growing happiness.

"It's very lucky," Bill said, "that you are a Zoroastrian. It makes it easier to talk to you."

"No luck involved, my son, just intelligent planning." The chaplain dropped some powdered Haoma into the flame, and Bill's nose twitched as the drugged incense filled the room. "By the grace of Ahura Mazdah I am an anointed priest of Zoroaster. By Allah's will a faithful muezzin of Islam, through

36

Yahweh's intercession a circumcized rabbi, and so forth." His benign face broke into a savage snarl. "And also because of an officer shortage I am the damned laundry officer." His face cleared. "But now, you must tell me your problem . . ."

"Well, it's not easy. It may be just foolish suspicion on my part, but I'm worried about one of my buddies. There is something strange about him. I'm not sure how to tell it . . ."

"Have confidence, my boy, and reveal your innermost feelings to me, and do not fear. What I hear shall never leave this room, for I am bound to secrecy by the oath of my calling. Unburden yourself."

"That's very nice of you, and I *do* feel better already. You see, this buddy of mine has always been a little funny, he shines the boots for all of us and volunteered for latrine orderly and doesn't like girls."

The chaplain nodded beatifically and fanned some of the incense toward his nose. "I see little here to worry you, he sounds a decent lad. For is it not written in the Vendidad that we should aid our fellow man and seek to shoulder his burdens and pursue not the harlots of the streets?"

Bill pouted. "That's all right for Sunday school, but it's no way to act in the troopers! Anyway, we just thought he was out of his mind, and he might have been—but that's not all. I was with him on the gun deck, and he pointed his watch at the guns and pressed the stem, and I heard it *click!* It could be a camera. I . . . I think he is a Chinger spy!" Bill sat back, breathing deeply and sweating. The fatal words had been spoken.

The chaplain continued to nod, smiling, half-unconscious from the Haoma fumes. Finally he snapped out of it, blew his nose, and opened the thick copy of the Avesta. He mumbled aloud in Old Persian a bit, which seemed to brace him, then slammed it shut.

"You must not bear false witness!" he boomed, fixing Bill with piercing gaze and accusing finger.

"You got me wrong," Bill moaned, writhing in the chair. "He's *done* these things, I *saw* him use the watch. What kind of spiritual aid do you call *this?*"

"Just a bracer, my boy, a touch of the old-time religion to renew your sense of guilt and start you thinking about going to church regular again. You have been backsliding!"

"What else could I do—chapel is forbidden during recruit training?"

"Circumstances are no excuse, but you will be forgiven this time because Ahura Mazdah is all-merciful."

"But what about my buddy—the spy?"

"You must forget your suspicions, for they are not worthy of a follower of Zoroaster. This poor lad must not suffer because of his natural inclinations to be friendly, to aid his comrades, to keep himself pure, to own a crummy watch that goes click. And besides, if you do not mind my introducing a spot of logic—how could he be a spy? To be a spy he would have to be a Chinger, and Chingers are seven feet tall with tails. Catch?"

"Yeah, yeah," Bill mumbled unhappily. "I could figure that one out for myself—but it still doesn't explain everything . . ."

"It satisfies me, and it must satisfy you. I feel that Ahriman has possessed you to make you think evil of your comrade, and you had better do some penance and join me in a quick prayer before the laundry officer comes back on duty."

This ritual was quickly finished, and Bill helped stow the things back in the box and watched it vanish back into the desk. He said good-by and turned to leave.

"Just one moment, my son," the chaplain said with his warmest smile, reaching back over his shoulder at the same time to grab the end of his necktie. He pulled, and his collar whirred about, and as it did the blissful expression was wiped from his face to be replaced by a surly snarl. "Just where do you think you're going, bowb! Put your ass back in that chair."

"B-but," Bill stammered, "you said I was dismissed."

"That's what the chaplain said, and as laundry officer I have no truck with him. Now—*fast*—what's the name of this Chinger spy you are hiding?"

"I told you about that under oath—"

"You told the *chaplain* about it, and he keeps his word and he didn't tell me, but I just happened to hear." He pressed a red button on the control panel. "The MPs are on the way. You talk before they get here, bowb, or I'll have you keel-hauled without a space suit and deprived of canteen privileges for a year. The name?"

"Eager Beager," Bill sobbed, as heavy feet trampled outside and two redhats forced their way into the tiny room.

"I have a spy for you boys," the laundry officer announced triumphantly, and the MPs grated their teeth, howled deep in their throats, and launched themselves through the air at Bill. He dropped under the assault of fists and clubs and was running with blood before the laundry officer could pull the overmuscled morons with their eyes not an inch apart off him.

"Not him . . ." the officer gasped, and threw Bill a towel to wipe off some of the blood. "This is our informant, the loyal, patriotic hero who ratted on his buddy by the name of Eager Beager, who we will now grab and chain so he car. be questioned. Let's go."

The MPs held Bill up between them, and by the time they had come to the fuse tenders' quarters the breeze from their swift passage had restored him a bit. The laundry officer opened the door just enough to poke in his head. "Hi, gang!" he called cheerily. "Is Eager Beager here?"

Eager looked up from the boot he was polishing, waving and grinning. "That's me—gee."

"Get him!" the laundry officer expostulated, jumping aside and pointing accusingly. Bill dropped to the floor as the MPs let go of him and thundered into the compartment. By the time he had staggered back to his feet Eager was pinioned, handcuffed and chained, hand and foot, but still grinning.

"Gee—you guys want some boots polished too?"

"No backtalk, you dirty spy," the laundry officer grated, and slapped him hard in the offensive grin. At least he tried to slap him in the offensive grin, but Beager opened his mouth and bit the hand that hit him, clamping down hard so that the officer could not get away. "He bit me!" the man howled, and tried desperately to pull free. Both MPs, each handcuffed to an arm of the prisoner, raised their clubs to give him a sound battering.

At this moment the top of Eager Beager's head flew open.

Happening at any other time, this would have been considered unusual, but happening at this moment it was spectacularly unusual, and they all, including Bill, gaped, as a seven-inch-high lizard climbed out of the open skull and jumped to the floor in which it made a sizable dent upon landing. It had four tiny arms, a long tail, a head like a baby alligator, and was bright green. It looked exactly like a Chinger except that it was seven inches tall instead of seven feet.

"All bowby humans have B.O.," it said, in a thin imitation of Eager Beager's voice. "Chingers can't sweat. Chingers forever!" It charged across the compartment toward Beager's bunk.

Paralysis prevailed. All of the fuse tenders who had witnessed the impossible events stood or sat as they had been, frozen with shock, eyes bulging like hard-boiled eggs. The laundry officer was pinioned by the teeth locked into his hand, while the two MPs struggled with the handcuffs that held them to the immobile body. Only Bill was free to move and, still dizzy from the beating, he bent over to grab the tiny creature. Small and powerful talons locked into his flesh, and he was pulled from his feet and went sailing through the air to crash against a bulkhead. "Gee—that's for you, you stoolie!" the minuscule voice squeaked.

Before anyone else could interfere, the lizardoid ran to Beager's pile of barracks bags and tore the topmost one open and dived inside. A high-pitched humming grew in volume an instant later, and from the bag emerged the bulletlike nose of a shining projectile. It pushed out until a tiny spaceship not two feet long floated in the compartment. Then it rotated about its vertical axis, stopping when it pointed at the bulkhead. The humming rose in pitch, and the ship suddenly shot forward and tore through the metal of the partition as if it had been no stronger than wet cardboard. There were other distant tearing sounds as it penetrated bulkhead after bulkhead until, with a rending clang, it crashed through the outer skin of the ship and escaped into space. There was the roar of air rushing into the void and the clamor of alarm bells.

"Well I'll be damned . . ." the laundry officer said, then snapped his gaping mouth closed and screamed, "Get this thing offa my hand—it's biting me to death!"

The two MPs still swayed back and forth, handcuffed effectively to the immobile figure of the former Eager Beager. Beager just stared, smiling around the grip he had on the officer's hand, and it wasn't until Bill got his atomic rifle and put the barrel into Eager's mouth and levered the jaw open that the hand could be withdrawn. While he did this Bill saw that the top of Eager's head had split open just above his ears and was held at the back by a shiny brass hinge. Inside the gaping skull, instead of brains and bones and things, was a model control room with a tiny chair, minuscule controls, TV screens, and a water cooler. Eager was just a robot worked by the little creature that had escaped in the spaceship. It looked like a Chinger—but it was only seven inches tall.

"Hey!" Bill said, "Eager is just a robot worked by the little creature that escaped in the spaceship! It looked like a Chinger—but it was only seven inches tall . . ."

"Seven inches, seven feet—what difference does it make!" the laundry officer mumbled petulantly as he wrapped a handkerchief around his wounded hand. "You don't expect us to tell the recruits how small the enemy really are, or to explain how they come from a 10G planet. We gotta keep the morale up."

V

Now that Eager Beager had turned out to be a Chinger spy,
Bill felt very much alone. Bowb Brown, who never talked
anyway, now talked even less, which meant never, so there
was no one that Bill could bitch to. Bowb was the only other
fuseman in the compartment who had been in Bill's squad
at Camp Leon Trotsky, and all of the new men were very
clannish and given to sitting close together and mumbling and
throwing suspicious looks over their shoulders if he should
come too close. Their only recreation was welding and every
off watch they would break out the welders and weld things
to the floor and the next watch cut them loose again, which
is about as dim a way of wasting time as there is; but they
seemed to enjoy it. So Bill was very much out of things and
tried bitching to Eager Beager.

"Look at the trouble you got me into!" he whined.

Beager just smiled back, unmoved by the complaint.

"At least close your head when I'm talking to you," Bill
snarled, and reached over to slam the top of Eager's head shut.
But it didn't do any good. Eager couldn't do anything any
more except smile. He had polished his last boot. He just
stood there now; he was really very heavy and besides was
magnetized to the floor, and the fuse tenders hung their dirty
shirts and arc welders on him. He stayed there for three
watches before someone figured out what to do with him,
until finally a squad of MPs came with crowbars and tilted
him into a handcar and rolled him away.

"So long," Bill called out, waving after him, then went

43

back to polishing his boots. "He was a good buddy, even if he was a Chinger spy."

Bowb didn't answer him, and welders wouldn't talk to him, and he spent a lot of the time avoiding Reverend Tembo. The grand old lady of the fleet, *Christine Keeler*, was still in orbit while her engines were being installed. There was very little to do, because, in spite of what First Class Spleen had said, they had mastered all the intricacies of fuse tending in a little less than the prescribed year; in fact it took them something like maybe fifteen minutes. In his free time Bill wandered around the ship, going as far as the MPs who guarded the hatchways would allow him, and even considered going back to see the chaplain so he could have someone to bitch to. But if he timed it wrong he might meet the laundry officer again, and that was more than he could face. So he walked through the ship, very much alone, and looked in through the door of a compartment and saw a boot on a bed.

Bill stopped, frozen, immobile, shocked, rigid, horrified, dismayed, and had to fight for control of his suddenly contracted bladder.

He knew that boot. He would never forget that boot until the day he died, just as he would never forget his serial number and could say it frontward or backward or from the inside out. Every detail of that terrible boot was clear in his memory, from the snakelike laces in the repulsive leather of the uppers—said to be made of human skin—to the corrugated stamping-soles tinged with red that could only have been human blood. That boot belonged to Deathwish Drang.

The boot was attached to a leg, and paralyzed with terror, as unable to control himself as a bird before a snake, he found himself leaning further and further into the compartment as his eyes traced up the leg past the belt to the shirt to the neck upon which rested the face that had featured

44

largely in his nightmares since he had enlisted. The lips moved . . .

"Is that you, Bill? C'mon in and rest it."

Bill stumbled in.

"Have a hunk of candy," Deathwish said, and smiled.

Reflex drove Bill's fingers into the offered box and set his jaw chewing on the first solid food that had passed his lips in weeks. Saliva spouted from dusty orifices, and his stomach gave a preliminary rumble, while his thoughts drove maddingly in circles as he tried to figure out what that expression was on Deathwish's face. Lips curved up at the corners behind the tusks, little crinkles on the cheeks. It was hopeless. He could not recognize it.

"I hear Eager Beager turned out to be a Chinger spy," Deathwish said, closing the box of candy and sliding it under the pillow. "I should have figured that one out myself. I knew there was something *very* wrong with him, doing his buddies' boots and that crap, but I thought he was just nuts. Should have known better . . ."

"Deathwish," Bill said hoarsely, "it can't be, I know—but you are acting like a human being!"

Deathwish chuckled, not his ripsaw-slicing-human-bone chuckle, but an almost normal one.

Bill stammered. "But you are a sadist, a pervert, a beast, a creature, a thing, a murderer . . ."

"Why, thanks, Bill. That's very nice to hear. I try to do my job to the best of my abilities, but I'm human enough to enjoy a word of praise now and then. Being a murderer is hard to project, but I'm glad it got across, even to a recruit as stupid as you were."

"B-but . . . aren't you *really* a . . ."

"Easy now!" Deathwish snapped, and there was enough of the old venom and vileness to lower Bill's body temperature six degrees. Then Deathwish smiled again. "Can't blame you, son, for carrying on this way, you being kind of stupid and from a rube planet and having your education retarded by the troopers and all that. But wake up, boy! Military education is far too important a thing to be wasted by allowing amateurs to get involved. If you read some of the things in our college textbooks it would make your blood run cold, yes indeed. Do you realize that in prehistoric times the drill sergeants, or whatever it was they called them, were *real* sadists! The armed forces would let these people with no real knowledge absolutely *destroy* recruits. Let them learn to hate the service before they learned to fear it, which plays hell with discipline. And talk about wasteful! They were always marching someone to death by accident or drowning a squad or nonsense like that. The waste alone would make you cry."

"Could I ask what you majored in in college?" Bill asked in a very tiny and humble voice.

"Military Discipline, Spirit-breaking, and Method Acting. A rough course, four years, but I graduated sigma cum, which is not bad for a boy from a working-class family. I've made a career of the service, and that's why I can't understand why the ungrateful bastards went and shipped me out on this crummy can!" He lifted his gold-rimmed glasses to flick away a developing tear.

"You expect gratitude from the service?" Bill asked humbly.

"No, of course not, how foolish of me. Thanks for jerking me back into line, Bill, you'll make a good trooper. All I expect is criminal indifference which I can take advantage of by working through the Old Boys Network, bribery, cutting false orders, black-marketing, and the other usual things. It's just that I *had* been doing a good job on you slobs in Camp Leon Trotsky, and the least I expected was to be left alone to keep doing it, which was pretty damn stupid of me. I had better get cracking on my transfer now." He slid to his feet and stowed the candy and gold-rimmed glasses away in a locked footlocker.

Bill, who in moments of shock found it hard to adjust instantly, was still bobbing his head and occasionally banging it with the heel of his hand. "Lucky thing," he said, "for your chosen career that you were born deformed—I mean you have such nice teeth."

"Luck nothing," Deathwish said, plunking one of his projecting tusks, "expensive as hell. Do you know what a gene-mutated, vat-grown, surgically-implanted set of two-inch tusks cost? I bet you don't know! I worked the summer vac for three years to earn enough to buy these—but I tell you they were worth it. The *image*, that's everything. I studied the old tapes of prehistoric spirit-breakers, and in their own crude way they were good. Selected by physical type and low I.Q. of course, but they knew their roles. Bulletheads, shaved clean, with scars, thick jaws, repulsive manners, hot pants, everything. I figured a small investment in the beginning would pay rich dividends in the end. And it was a sacrifice, believe me, you won't see many implanted tusks around! For a lot of reasons. Oh, maybe they are good for eating tough meat, but what the hell else? Wait until you try kissing your first girl . . . Now, get lost, Bill, I got things to do. See you around . . ."

His last words faded in the distance, since Bill's well-conditioned reflexes had carried him down the corridor the instant he had been dismissed. When the spontaneous terror faded, he began to walk with a crafty roll, like a duck with a sprung kneecap, that he thought looked like an old space-sailor's gait. He was beginning to feel a seasoned hand and momentarily labored under the delusion that he knew more about the troopers than they knew about him. This pathetic misconception was dispelled instantly by the speakers on the ceiling, which belched and then grated their nasal voices throughout the ship.

"Now hear this, the orders direct from the Old Man himself, Captain Zekial, that you all have been waiting to hear. We're heading into action, so we are going to have a clean buckle-down fore and aft, stow all loose gear."

A low, heartfelt groan of pain echoed from every compartment of the immense ship.

VI

There was plenty of latrine rumor and scuttlebutt about this first flight of the *Chris Keeler*, but none of it was true. The rumors were planted by undercover MPs and were valueless. About the only thing they could be sure of was that they might be going someplace because they seemed to be getting ready to go someplace. Even Tembo admitted to that as they lashed down fuses in the storeroom.

"Then again," he added, "we might be doing all this just to fool any spies into thinking we are going someplace, when really some other ships are going there."

"Where?" Bill asked irritably, tying his forefinger into a knot and removing part of the nail when he pulled it free.

"Why anyplace at all, it doesn't matter." Tembo was undisturbed by anything that did not bear on his faith. "But I do know where *you* are going, Bill."

"Where?" Eagerly. A perennial sucker for a rumor.

"Straight to hell unless you are saved."

"Not again . . ." Bill pleaded.

"Look there," Tembo said temptingly, and projected a heavenly scene with golden gates, clouds, and a soft tom-tom beat in the background.

"Knock off that salvation crap!" First Class Spleen shouted, and the scene vanished.

Something tugged slightly at Bill's stomach, but he ignored it as being just another of the symptoms sent up continually by his panic-stricken gut, which thought it was starving to death and hadn't yet realized that all its marvelous grinding and dissolving machinery had been condemned to a liquid diet. But Tembo stopped work and cocked his head to one side, then poked himself experimentally in the stomach.

"We're moving," he said positively, "and going interstellar too. They've turned on the star-drive."

"You mean we are breaking through into sub-space and will soon experience the terrible wrenching at every fiber of our being?"

"No, they don't use the old sub-space drive any more, because though a lot of ships broke through into sub-space with a fiber-wrenching jerk, none of them have yet broke back out. I read in the *Trooper's Times* where some mathematician said that there had been a slight error in the equations and that time was different in sub-space, but it was different faster not different slower, so that it will be maybe forever before those ships come out."

"Then we're going into hyper-space?"

"No such thing."

"Or we're being dissolved into our component atoms and recorded in the memory of a giant computor who thinks we are somewhere else so there we are?"

"Wow!" Tembo said, his eyebrows crawling up to his hairline. "For a Zoroastrian farm boy you have some strange ideas! Have you been smoking or drinking something I don't know about?"

"Tell me!" Bill pleaded. "If it's not one of them—what is it? We're going to have to cross interstellar space to fight the Chingers. How are we going to do it?"

"It's like this." Tembo looked around to make sure that First Class Spleen was out of sight, then put his cupped hands together to form a ball. "You make believe that my hands are the ship, just floating in space. Then the Bloater Drive is turned on—"

"The *what?*"

"The Bloater Drive. It's called that because it bloats things up. You know, everything is made up of little bitty things called electrons, protons, neutrons, trontrons, things like that, sort of held together by a kind of binding energy. Now, if you weaken the energy that holds things together— I forgot to tell you that also they are spinning around all the time like crazy, or maybe you already knew—you weaken the energy, and because they are going around so fast all the little pieces start to move away from each other, and the weaker the energy the farther apart they move. Are you with me so far?"

"I think I am, but I'm not sure that I like it."

"Keep cool. Now—see my hands? As the energy gets weaker the ship gets bigger," he moved his hands further apart. "It gets bigger and bigger until it is as big as a planet, then as big as a sun then a whole stellar system. The Bloater Drive can make us just as big as we want to be, then it's turned the other way and we shrink back to our regular size and there we are."

"*Where* are we?"

"Wherever we want to be," Tembo answered patiently.

Bill turned away and industriously rubbed shine-o onto a fuse as First Class Spleen sauntered by, a suspicious glint in his eye. As soon as he had turned the corner, Bill leaned over and hissed at Tembo.

"How can we be anywhere else than where we started? Getting bigger, getting smaller doesn't get us anyplace."

"Well, they're pretty tricky with the old Bloater Drive. The way I heard it it's like you take a rubber band and hold one end in each hand. You don't move your left hand, but you stretch the band out as far as it will go with your right hand. When you let the band shrink back again you keep your right hand steady and let go with your left. See? You never moved the rubber band, just stretched it and let it snap—but it has moved over. Like our ship is doing now. It's getting bigger, but in one direction. When the nose reaches wherever we are going the stern will be wherever we were. Then we shrink, and bango! there we are. And you can get into heaven just that easily, my son, if only . . ."

"Preaching on government time, Tembo!" First Class Spleen howled from the other side of the fuse rack over which he was looking with a mirror tied to the end of a rod. "I'll have you polishing fuse clips for a year. You've been warned before."

They tied and polished in silence after that, until the little planet about as big as a tennis ball swam in through the bulkhead. A perfect little planet with tiny icecaps, cold fronts, cloud cover, oceans, and the works.

"What's that?" Bill yiped.

"Bad navigation," Tembo scowled. "Backlash, the ship is slipping back a little on one end instead of going all the other way. No-no! Don't touch it, it can cause accidents sometimes. That's the planet we just left, Phigerinadon II."

"My home," Bill sobbed, and felt the tears rise as the planet shrank to the size of a marble. "So long, Mom." He waved as the marble shrank to a mote, then vanished.

After this the journey was uneventful, particularly since they could not feel when they were moving, did not know when they stopped, and had no idea where they were. Though they were sure they had arrived somewhere when they were ordered to strip the lashings from the fuses. The inaction continued for three watches, and then the General Quarters alarm sounded. Bill ran with the others, happy for the first time since he had enlisted. All the sacrifices, the hardships would not be in vain. He was seeing action at last against the dirty Chingers.

They stood in first position opposite the fuse racks, eyes intent on the red bands on the fuses that were called the fusebands. Through the soles of his boots Bill could feel a faint, distant tremor in the deck.

"What's that?" he asked Tembo out of the corner of his mouth.

"Main drive, not the Bloater Drive. Atomic engines. Means we must be maneuvering, doing something."

"But *what?*"

"Watch them fusebands!" First Class Spleen shouted.

Bill was beginning to sweat—then suddenly realized that it was becoming excruciatingly hot. Tembo, without taking his eyes from the fuses, slipped out of his clothes and folded them neatly behind him.

"Are we allowed to do that?" Bill asked, pulling at his collar. "What's happening?"

"It's against regulations, but you have to strip or cook. Peel, son, or you will die unblessed. We must be going into action because the shields are up. Seventeen force screens, one electromagnetic screen, a double-armored hull, and a thin layer of pseudo-living jelly that flows over and seals any openings. With all that stuff there is absolutely no energy loss from the ship, nor any way to get rid of energy. Or heat. With the engines running and everyone sweating it can get pretty hot. Even hotter when the guns fire."

The temperature stayed high, just at the boundary of tolerability for hours, while they stared at the fusebands. At one point there was a tiny plink that Bill felt through his bare feet on the hot metal rather than heard.

"And what was that?"

"Torpedoes being fired."

"At *what?*"

Tembo just shrugged in answer and never let his vigilant gaze stray from the fusebands. Bill writhed with frustration, boredom, heat rash, and fatigue for another hour, until the all clear blew and a breath of cool air came in from the ventilators. By the time he had pulled his uniform back on Tembo was gone, and he trudged wearily back to his quarters.

There was a new mimeographed notice pinned to the bulletin board in the corridor and he bent to read its blurred message.

FROM: Captain Zekial
TO: All Personnel
RE: Recent engagement

On 23/11-8956 this ship did participate in the destruction by atomic torpedo of the enemy installation 17KL-345 and did in concert with the other vessels of said flotilla *Red Crutch* accomplish its mission, it is thereby hereby authorized that all personnel of this vessel shall attach an Atomic Cluster to the ribbon denoting the Active Duty Unit Engagement Award, or however if this is their first mission of this type they will be authorized to wear the Unit Engagement Award.

NOTE: Some personnel have been observed with their Atomic Clusters inverted and this is WRONG and a COURTS-MARTIAL OFFENSE that is punishable by DEATH.

VII

After the heroic razing of 17KL-345 there were weeks of training and drill to restore the battle-weary veterans to their usual fitness. But midway in these depressing months a new call sounded over the speakers, one Bill had never heard before, a clanging sound like steel bars being clashed together in a metal drum full of marbles. It meant nothing to him nor to the other new men, but it sent Tembo springing from his bunk to do a quick two-step Death Curse Dance with tom-tom accompaniment on his footlocker cover.

"Are you around the bend?" Bill asked dully from where he sprawled and read a tattered copy of *Real Ghoul Sex Fiend Shocker Comics with Built-in Sound Effects*. A ghastly moan was keening from the page he was looking at.

"Don't you know?" Tembo asked. "Don't you KNOW! That's mail call, my boy, the grandest sound in space."

The rest of the watch was spent in hurrying up and waiting, standing in line, and all the rest. Maximum inefficiency was attached to the delivery of the mail, but finally, in spite of all barriers, the post was distributed and Bill had a precious spacial-postal from his mother. On one side of the card was a picture of the Noisome-Offal refinery just outside of his home town, and this alone was enough to raise a lump in his throat. Then, in the tiny square allowed for the message, his mother's pathetic scrawl had traced out: "Bad crop, in debt, robmule has packing glanders, hope you are the same—love, Maw." Still, it was a message from home, and he read and reread it as they stood in line for chow. Tembo, just ahead of him, also had a card, all angels and churches, just what you would expect, and Bill was shocked when he saw Tembo read the card one last time then plunge it into his cup of dinner.

"What are you doing that for?" he asked, shocked.

"What else is mail good for?" Tembo hummed, and poked the card deeper. "You just watch this now."

Before Bill's startled gaze, and right in front of his eyes, the card was starting to swell. The white surface broke off and fell away in tiny flakes while the brown insides grew and grew until they filled the cup and were an inch thick. Tembo fished the dripping slab out and took a large bite from one corner.

"Dehydrated chocolate," he said indistinctly. "Good! Try yours."

Even before he spoke Bill had pushed his card down into the liquid and was fascinatedly watching it swell. The message fell away, but instead of brown a swelling white mass became visible.

"Taffy—or bread maybe," he said, and tried not to drool.

The white mass was swelling, pushing against the sides of the cup, expanding out of the top. Bill grabbed the end and held it as it rose. Out and out it came until every drop of liquid had been absorbed and Bill held between his out-stretched hands a string of fat, connected letters over two yards long. VOTE—FOR—HONEST—GEEK—THE—TROOPERS'—FRIEND they read. Bill leaned over and bit out an immense mouthful of T. He spluttered and spat the damp shards onto the deck.

"Cardboard," he said sadly. "Mother always shops for bargains. Even in dehydrated chocolate . . ." He reached for his cup for something to wash the old-newsprint taste out of his mouth, but it was empty.

Somewhere high in the seats of power, a decision was made, a problem resolved, an order issued. From small things do big things grow; a tiny bird turd lands on a snow-covered mountain slope, rolls, collects snow, becomes bigger and bigger, gigantic and more gigantic until it is a thundering mass of snow and ice, an avalanche, a ravening mass of hurtling death that wipes out an entire village. From small beginnings . . . Who knows what the beginning was here, perhaps the Gods do, but they are laughing. Perhaps the haughty, strutting peahen wife of some High Minister saw a bauble she cherished and with shrewish, spiteful tongue exacerbated her peacock husband until, to give himself peace, he promised her the trinket, then sought the money for its purchase. Perhaps this was a word in the Emperor's ear about a new campaign in the 77sub7th Zone, quiet now for years, a victory there—or even a draw if there were enough deaths—would mean a medal, an award, some cash. And thus did a woman's covetousness, like a tiny bird's turd, start the snowball of warfare rolling, mighty fleets gathering, ship after ship assembling, like a rock in a pool of water the ripples spread until even the lowliest were touched by its motion . . .

"We're heading for action," Tembo said as he sniffed at his cup of lunch. "They're loading up the chow with stimulants, pain depressors, saltpeter, and antibiotics."

"Is that why they keep playing the patriotic music?" Bill shouted so that he could be heard over the endless roar of bugles and drums that poured from the speakers. Tembo nodded.

"There is little time left to be saved, to assure your place in Samedi's legions—"

"Why don't you talk to Bowb Brown?" Bill screamed. "I got tom-toms coming out of my ears! Every time I look at a wall I see angels floating by on clouds. Stop bothering me!

57

Work on Bowb—anybody who would do what he does with thoats would probably join up with your Voodoo mob in a second."

"I have talked with Brown about his soul, but the issue is still in doubt. He never answers me, so I am not sure if he has heard me or not. But you are different, my son, you show anger, which means you are showing doubt, and doubt is the first step to belief . . ."

The music cut off in mid-peal, and for three seconds there was an echoing blast of silence that abruptly terminated.

"Now hear this. Attention all hands . . . stand by . . . in a few moments we will be taking you to the flagship for a on-the-spot report from the admiral . . . stand by . . ." The voice was cut off by the sounding of General Quarters but went on again when this hideous sound had ended. ". . . and here we are on the bridge of that gigantic conquistadore of the spacelanes, the twenty-mile-long, heavily armored, mightily gunned super battleship the *Fairy Queen* . . . the men on watch are stepping aside now and coming toward me in a simple uniform of spun platinum is the Grand Admiral of the Fleet, the Right Honorable Lord Archaeopteryx . . . Could you spare us a moment Your Lordship? Wonderful! The next voice you hear will be . . ."

The next voice was a burst of music while the fusemen eyed their fusebands, but the next voice after that had all the rich adenoidal tones always heard from peers of the Empire.

"Lads—we're going into action! This, the mightiest fleet the galaxy has ever seen is heading directly toward the enemy to deliver the devastating blow that may win us the war. In my operations tank before me I see a myriad pinpoints of light, stretching as far as the eye can see, and each point of light—I tell you they are like holes in a blanket!—is not a ship,

58

not a squadron—but an entire *fleet!* We are sweeping forward, closing in . . ."

The sound of tom-toms filled the air, and on the fuseband that Bill was watching appeared a matched set of golden gates, swinging open.

"Tembo!" he screamed. "Will you knock that off! I want to hear about the battle . . ."

"Canned tripe," Tembo sniffed. "Better to use the few remaining moments of this life that may remain to you to seek salvation. That's no admiral, that's a canned tape. I've heard it five times already, and they only play it to build morale before what they are sure is to be a battle with heavy losses. It never *was* an admiral, it's from an old TV program . . ."

"Yippee!" Bill shouted, and leaped forward. The fuse he was looking at crackled with a brilliant discharge around the clips, and at the same moment the fuseband charred and turned from red to black. "Unggh!" he grunted, then "Unggh! Unggh! Unggh!" in rapid succession, burning his palms on the still hot fuse, dropping it on his toe, and finally getting it into a fuseway. When he turned back Tembo had already clipped a fresh fuse into the empty clips.

"That was *my* fuse—you shouldn't have . . ." there were tears in his eyes.

"Sorry. But by the rules I must help if I am free."

"Well, at least we're in action," Bill said, back in position and trying to favor his bruised foot.

"Not in action yet, still too cold in here. And that was just a fuse breakdown, you can tell by the clip discharge, they do that sometimes when they get old."

". . . massed armadas manned by heroic troopers . . ."

"We *could* have been in combat." Bill pouted.

". . . thunder of atomic broadsides and lightning trails of hurtling torpedoes . . ."

"I think we are now. It does feel warmer, doesn't it, Bill?

We had better undress; if it really is a battle we may get too busy."

"Let's go, let's go, down to the buff," First Class Spleen barked, leaping gazellelike down the rows of fuses, clad only in a pair of dirty gym socks and his tattooed-on stripes and fouled-fuse insignia of rank. There was a sudden crackling in the air, and Bill felt the clipped-short stubs of his hair stirring in his scalp.

"What's that?" he yiped.

"Secondary discharge from that bank of fuses," Tembo pointed. "It's classified as to what is happening, but I heard tell that it means one of the defense screens is under radiation attack, and as it overloads it climbs up the spectrum to green, to blue to ultraviolet until finally it goes black and the screen breaks down."

"That sounds pretty way out."

"I told you it was just a rumor. The material is classified . . ."

"THERE SHE GOES!!"

A crackling bang split the humid air of the fuse room, and a bank of fuses arced, smoked, burned black. One of them cracked in half, showering small fragments like shrapnel in every direction. The fusemen leaped, grabbed the fuses, slipped in replacements with sweating hands, barely visible to each other through the reeking layers of smoke. The fuses were driven home, and there was a moment's silence, broken only by a plaintive bleating from the communications screen.

"Son of a bowb!" First Class Spleen muttered, kicking a fuse out of the way and diving for the screen. His uniform jacket was hanging on a hook next to it, and he struggled into this before banging the RECEIVE switch. He finished closing the last button just as the screen cleared. Spleen saluted, so it must have been an officer he was facing; the screen was edge-on to Bill, so he couldn't tell, but the voice had the

quacking no-chin-and-plenty-of-teeth whine that he was beginning to associate with the officer class.

"You're slow in answering, First Class Spleen—maybe
Second Class Spleen would be able to answer faster?"

"Have pity, sir—I'm an old man." He dropped to his knees
in a prayerful attitude which took him off the screen.

"Get up, you idiot! Have you repaired the fuses after that
last overload?"

"We *replace*, sir, not *repair* . . ."

"None of your technical gibberish, you swine! A straight
answer!"

"All in order, sir. Operating in the green. No complaints
from anyone, your worship."

"Why are you out of uniform?"

"I am in uniform, sir," Spleen whined, moving closer to
the screen so that his bare behind and shaking lower limbs
could not be seen.

"Don't lie to me! There's *sweat* on your forehead. You
aren't allowed to sweat in uniform. Do you see me sweating?
And I have a cap on too—at the correct angle. I'll forget it
this time because I have a heart of gold. Dismissed."

"Filthy bowb!" Spleen cursed at the top of his lungs, tearing the jacket from his stifling body. The temperature was
over 120 and still rising. "Sweat! They have air conditioning
on the bridge—and where do you think they discharge the
heat? In here! YEEOOW!!"

Two entire banks of fuses blew out at the same time, three
of the fuses exploding like bombs. At the same moment the
floor under their feet bucked hard enough to actually be felt.

"Big trouble!" Tembo shouted. "Anything that is strong
enough to feel through the stasis field must be powerful
enough to flatten this ship like a pancake. There go some
more!" He dived for the bank and kicked a fuse clear of the
clips and jammed in a replacement.

It was an inferno. Fuses were exploding like aerial bombs, sending whistling particles of ceramic death through the air. There was a lightning crackle as a board shorted to the metal floor and a hideous scream, thankfully cut short, as the sheet of lightning passed through a fuse tender's body. Greasy smoke boiled and hung in sheets, making it almost impossible to see. Bill raked the remains of a broken fuse from the darkened clips and jumped for the replacement rack. He clutched the ninety-pound fuse in his aching arms and had just turned back toward the boards, when the universe exploded . . .

All the remaining fuses seemed to have shorted at once, and the screaming bolt of crackling electricity crashed the length of the room. In its eye-piercing light and in a single, eternal moment Bill saw the flame sear through the ranks of the fuse tenders, throwing them about and incinerating them like particles of dust in an open fire. Tembo crumpled and collapsed, a mass of seared flesh; a flying length of metal tore First Class Spleen open from neck to groin in a single hideous wound.

"Look at that vent in Spleen!" Bowb shouted, then screamed as a ball of lightning rolled over him and turned him to a blackened husk in a fraction of a second.

By chance, a mere accident, Bill was holding the solid bulk of the fuse before him when the flame struck. It washed over his left arm, which was on the outside of the fuse, and hurled its flaming weight against the thick cylinder. The force hit Bill, knocked him back toward the reserve racks of fuses, and rolled him end over end flat on the floor while the all-destroying sheet of fire crackled inches above his head. It died away as suddenly as it had come, leaving behind nothing but smoke, heat, the scorched smell of roasted flesh, destruction, and death, death, death. Bill crawled painfully for the hatchway, and nothing else moved down the blackened and twisted length of the fuse room.

The compartment below seemed just as hot, its air as bereft of nourishment for his lungs as the one he had just quitted. He crawled on, barely conscious of the fact that he moved on two lacerated knees and one bloody hand. His other arm just hung and dragged, a twisted and blackened length of debris, and only the blessings of deep shock kept him from screaming with unbearable pain.

He crawled on, over a sill, through a passageway. The air was clearer here and much cooler: he sat up and inhaled its blessed freshness. The compartment was familiar—yet unfamiliar—he blinked at it, trying to understand why. Long and narrow, with a curved wall that had the butt ends of immense guns projecting from it. The main battery, of course, the guns Chinger spy Eager Beager had photographed. Different now, the ceiling closer to the deck, bent and dented, as if some gigantic hammer had beat on it from the outside. There was a man slumped in the gunner's seat of the nearest weapon.

"What happened?" Bill asked, dragging himself over to the man and clutching him by the shoulder. Surprisingly enough the gunner only weighed a few pounds, and he fell from the seat, light as a husk, with a shriveled parchment face as though not a drop of liquid were left in his body.

"Dehydrator Ray," Bill grunted. "I thought they only had them on TV." The gunner's seat was padded and looked very comfortable, far more so than the warped steel deck: Bill slid into the recently vacated position and stared with unseeing eyes at the screen before him. Little moving blobs of light.

In large letters, just above the screen, was printed: GREEN LIGHTS OUR SHIPS, RED LIGHTS ENEMY. FORGETTING THIS IS A COURTS-MARTIAL OFFENSE. "I won't forget," Bill mumbled, as he started to slide sideways from the chair. To steady himself he grabbed a large handle that rose before him, and when he did a circle of light with an X in it moved on the screen. It was very interesting. He put the circle around one of the green lights, then remembered something about a courts-martial offense. He jiggled it a bit, and it moved over to a red light, with the X right over the light. There was a red button on top of the handle, and he pressed it because it looked like the kind of button that is made to be pressed. The gun next to him went *whffle* . . . in a very subdued way, and the red light went out. Not very interesting; he let go of the handle.

"Oh, but you are a fighting fool!" a voice said, and, with some effort, Bill turned his head. A man stood in the doorway wearing a burned and tattered uniform still hung with shreds of gold braid. He weaved forward. "I saw it," he breathed. "Until my dying day I won't forget it. A fighting fool! What guts! Fearless! Forward against the enemy, no holds barred, don't give up the ship . . ."

"What the bowb you talking about?" Bill asked thickly.

"A hero!" the officer said, pounding Bill on the back; this caused a great deal of pain and was the last straw for his conscious mind, which let go the reins of command and went away to sulk. Bill passed out.

VIII

"Now won't you be a nice trooper-wooper and drink your dinner . . ."

The warm notes of the voice insinuated themselves into a singularly repulsive dream that Bill was only too glad to leave, and, with a great deal of effort, he managed to heave his eyes open. A quick bit of blinking got them into focus, and he saw before him a cup on a tray held by a white hand attached to a white arm connected to a white uniform well stuffed with female breasts. With a guttural animal growl Bill knocked the tray aside and hurled himself at the dress. He didn't make it, because his left arm was wrapped up in something and hung from wires, so that he spun around in the bed like an impaled beetle, still uttering harsh cries. The nurse shrieked and fled.

"Glad to see that you are feeling better," the doctor said, whipping him straight in the bed with a practiced gesture and numbing Bill's still flailing right arm with a neat judo blow. "I'll pour you some more dinner, and you drink it right down, then we'll let your buddies in for the unveiling, they're all waiting outside."

The tingling was dying from his arm, and he could wrap his fingers about the cup now. He sipped. "What buddies? What unveiling? What's going on here?" he asked suspiciously.

Then the door was opened, and the troopers came in. Bill searched their faces, looking for buddies, but all he saw were ex-welders and strangers. Then he remembered. "Bowb Brown cooked!" he screamed. "Tembo broiled! First Class

65

Spleen gutted! They're all dead!" He hid under the covers and moaned horribly.

"That's no way for a hero to act," the doctor said, dragging him back onto the pillows and tucking the covers under his arms. "You're a hero, trooper, the man whose guts, ingenuity, integrity, stick-to-itiveness, fighting spirit, and deadly aim saved the ship. All the screens were down, the power room destroyed, the gunners dead, control lost, and the enemy dreadnaught zeroing in for the kill when you appeared like an avenging angel, wounded and near to death, and with your last conscious effort fired the shot heard round the fleet, the single blast that disemboweled the enemy and saved our ship, the grand old lady of the fleet, *Christine Keeler*." He handed a sheet of paper to Bill. "I am of course quoting from the official report; me myself, I think it was just a lucky accident."

"You're just jealous," Bill sneered, already falling in love with his new image.

"Don't get Freudian with me!" the doctor screamed, then snuffled pitifully. "I always wanted to be a hero, but all I do is wait hand and foot on heroes. I'm taking that bandage off now."

He unclipped the wires that held up Bill's arm and began to unwind the bandages while the troopers crowded around to watch.

"How is my arm, Doc?" Bill was suddenly worried.

"Grilled like a chop. I had to cut it off."

"Then what is this?" Bill shrieked, horrified.

"Another arm that I sewed on. There were lots of them left over after the battle. The ship had over 42 per cent casualties, and I was really cutting and chopping and sewing, I tell you."

The last bandage fell away and the troopers ahhhed with delight.

"Say, that's a mighty fine arm!"

"Make it do something."

"And a damn nice seam there at the shoulder—look how neat the stitches are!"

"Plenty of muscles, too, and good and long, not like the crummy little short one he has on the other side."

"Longer and darker—that's a great skin color!"

"It's Tembo's arm!" Bill howled. "Take it away!" He squirmed across the bed but the arm came after him. They propped him up again on the pillows.

"You're a lucky bowb, Bill, having a good arm like that. And your buddy's arm too."

"We know that he wanted you to have it."

"You'll always have something to remember him by."

It really wasn't a bad arm. Bill bent it and flexed the fingers, still looking at it suspiciously. It felt all right. He reached out with it and grabbed a trooper's arm and squeezed. He could feel the man's bones grating together while he screamed and writhed. Then Bill looked closer at the hand and began to shout curses at the doctor.

"You stupid sawbones! You thoat doctor! Some big job— this is a *right arm!*"

"So it's a right arm—so what?"

"But you cut off my *left* arm! Now I have two right arms . . ."

"Listen, there was a shortage of left arms. I'm no miracle worker. I do my best and all I get are complaints. Be happy I didn't sew on a leg." He leered evilly. "Or even better I didn't sew on a . . ."

"It's a good arm, Bill," said the trooper who was rubbing his recently crushed forearm. "And you're really lucky too. Now you can salute with either arm, no one else can do that."

"You're right," Bill said humbly. "I never thought of that. I'm really very lucky." He tried a salute with his left-right arm, and the elbow whipped up nicely and the fingertips quivered at his eyebrow. All the troopers snapped to attention and returned the salute. The door crashed open, and an officer poked his head in.

"Stand easy, men—this is just an informal visit by the Old Man."

"Captain Zekial coming here!"

"I've never seen the Old Man . . ." The troopers chippered like birds and were as nervous as virgins at a defloration ceremony. Three more officers came through the door and finally a male nurse leading a ten-year-old moron wearing a bib and a captain's uniform.

"Uhh . . . hi ya fellows . . ." the captain said.

"The captain wishes to pay his respects to you all," the first lieutenant said crisply.

"Is dat da guy in da bed . . . ?"

"And particularly wishes to pay his personal respects to the hero of the hour."

". . . Dere was sometin' else but I forgot . . ."

"And he furthermore wishes to inform the valiant fighter who saved our ship that he is being raised in grade to Fuse Tender First Class, which increase in rank includes an automatic re-enlistment for seven years to be added to his original enlistment, and that upon dismissal from the hospital he is to go by first available transportation to the Imperial Planet of Helior, there to receive the hero's award of the Purple Dart with Coalsack Nebula Cluster from the Emperor's own hand."

". . . I think I gotta go to da bathroom . . ."

"But now the exigencies of command recall him to the bridge, and he wishes you all an affectionate farewell."

Bill saluted with both arms, and the troopers stood at attention until the captain and his officers had gone, then the doctor dismissed the troopers as well.

"Isn't the Old Man a little young for his post?" Bill asked.

"Not as young as some," the doctor scratched through his hypodermic needles looking for a particularly dull one for an injection. "You have to remember that all captains have to be of the nobility and even a large nobility gets stretched damn thin over a galactic empire. We take what we can get." He found a crooked needle and clipped it to the cylinder.

"Affirm, so he's young, but isn't he also a little stupid for the job?"

"Watch that lese-majesty stuff, bowb! You get an empire that's a couple of thousand years old, and you get a nobility that keeps inbreeding, and you get some of the crunched genes and defective recessives coming out and you got a group of people that are a little more exotic than most nut houses. There's nothing wrong with the Old Man that a new I.Q. wouldn't cure! You should have seen the captain of the last ship I was on . . ." he shuddered and jabbed the needle viciously into Bill's flesh. Bill screamed, then gloomily watched the blood drip from the hole after the hypodermic had been withdrawn.

The door closed, and Bill was alone, looking at the blank wall and his future. He was a Fuse Tender First Class, and that was nice. But the compulsory re-enlistment for seven years was not so nice. His spirits dropped. He wished he could talk to some of his old buddies, then remembered that they were all dead, and his spirits dropped even further. He tried to cheer himself up but could think of nothing to be cheery about until he discovered that he could shake hands with himself. This made him feel a little bit better.

He lay back on the pillows and shook hands with himself until he fell asleep.

Book Two

A DIP IN THE
SWIMMING-POOL REACTOR

I

Ahead of them the front end of the cylindrical shuttleship was a single, gigantic viewport, a thick shield of armored glass now filled by the rushing coils of cloud that they were dropping down through. Bill leaned back comfortably in the deceleration chair, watching the scene with keen anticipation. There were seats for twenty in the stubby shuttleship, but only three of them, including Bill's, were now occupied. Sitting next to him, and he tried hard not to look too often, was a gunner first class who looked as though he had been blown out of one of his own guns. His face was mostly plastic and contained just a single, bloodshot eye. He was a mobile basket case, since his four missing limbs had been replaced by glistening gadgetry, all shining pistons, electronic controls, and coiling wires. His gunner's insignia was welded to the steel frame that took the place of his upper arm. The third man, a thickset brute of an infantry sergeant, had fallen asleep as soon as they boarded after transshipping from the stellar transport.

"Bowbidy-bowb! Look at that!" Bill felt elated as their ship broke through the clouds and there, spread before them, was the gleaming golden sphere of Helior, the Imperial Planet, the ruling world of 10,000 suns.

"What an albedo," the gunner grunted from somewhere inside his plastic face. "Hurts the eye."

"I should hope so! Solid gold—can you imagine—a planet plated with solid gold?!"

"No, I can't imagine. And I don't believe it either. It

73

would cost too much. But I can imagine one covered with anodized aluminum. Like that one."

Now that Bill looked closer he could see that it didn't *really* shine like gold, and he started to feel depressed again. No! He forced himself to perk up. You could take away the gold but you couldn't take away the glory! Helior was still the imperial world, the never sleeping, all-seeing eye in the heart of the galaxy. Everything that happened on every planet or on every ship in space was reported here, sorted, coded, filed, annotated, judged, lost, found, acted on. From Helior came the orders that ruled the worlds of man, that held back the night of alien domination. Helior, a man-changed world with its seas, mountains, and continents covered by a shielding of metal, miles thick, layer upon layer of levels with a global population dedicated to but one ideal. Rule. The gleaming upper level was dotted with space ships of all sizes, while the dark sky twinkled with others arriving and departing. Closer and closer swam the scene, then there was a sudden burst of light and the window went dark.

"We crashed!" Bill gasped. "Good as dead . . ."

"Shut your wug. That was just the film what broke. Since there's no brass on this run they won't bother fixing it."

"Film—?"

"What else? Are you so ratty in the head you think they're going to build shuttleships with great big windows in the nose just where the maximum friction on re-entry will burn holes in them? A film. Back projection. For all we know it's nighttime here."

The pilot mashed them with 15G when they landed (he also knew he had no brass on this run), and while they were popping their dislocated vertebrae back into position and squeezing their eyeballs back into shape so that they could see, the hatch swung open. Not only was it night, but it was raining too. A Second-class Passenger Handler's Mate poked his head in and swept them with a professionally friendly grin.

"Welcome to Helior, Imperial Planet of a thousand delights—" his face fell into a habitual snarl. "Ain't there no officers with you bowbs? C'mon, shag outta there, get the uranium out, we gotta schedule to keep."

They ignored him as he brushed by and went to wake the infantry sergeant, still snoring like a broken impeller, untroubled in his sleep by a little thing like 15Gs. The snore changed to a throaty grunt that was cut into by the Passenger Handler's Mate's shrill scream as he was kneed in the groin. Still muttering, the sergeant joined them as they left the ship and he helped steady the gunner's clattering metal legs on the still wet surface of the landing ramp. They watched with stony resignation as their duffel bags were ejected from the luggage compartment into a deep pool of water. As a last feeble flick of petty revenge the Passenger Handler's Mate turned off the repeller field that had been keeping the rain off them, and they were soaking wet in an instant and chilled by the icy wind. They shouldered their bags—except for the gunner, who dragged his on little wheels—and started for the nearest lights, at least a mile away and barely visible through the lashing rain. Halfway there the gunner froze up as his relays shorted, so they put the wheels under his heels and loaded the bags onto his legs, and he made a damn fine handcar the rest of the way.

"I make a damn fine handcar," the gunner growled.

"Don't bitch," the sergeant told him. "At least you got a civilian occupation." He kicked the door open and they walked and rolled into the welcome warmth of the operations office.

"You have a can of solvent?" Bill asked the man behind the counter.

"You have travel orders?" the man asked, ignoring his question.

"In my bag I got a can," the gunner said, and Bill pulled it open and rummaged around.

They handed over their orders; the gunner's were buttoned into his breast pocket, and the clerk fed them into the slot of the giant machine behind him. The machine hummed and flashed lights, and Bill dripped solvent onto all of the gunner's electrical connections until the water was washed away. A horn sounded, the orders were regurgitated, and a length of printed tape began clicking out of another orifice. The clerk snatched it up and read it rapidly.

"You're in trouble," he said with sadistic relish. "All three of you are supposed to get the Purple Dart in a ceremony with the Emperor and they're filming in three hours. You'll never make it in time."

"None of your bowb," the sergeant grated. "We just got off the ship. Where do we go?"

"Area 1457-D, Level K9, Block 823-7, Corridor 492, Chambers FLM-34, Room 62, ask for Producer Ratt."

"How do we get there?" Bill asked.

"Don't ask me, I just work here." The clerk threw three thick volumes onto the counter, each one over a foot square and almost as thick, with a chain riveted to the spine. "Find your own way, here's your floor plan, but you have to sign for it. Losing it is a courts-martial offense punishable by . . ."

The clerk suddenly realized that he was alone in the room with the three veterans, and as he blanched white he reached out for a red button. But before his finger could touch it the gunner's metal arm, spitting sparks and smoking, pinned it to the counter. The sergeant leaned over until his face was an inch from the clerk's, then spoke in a low, chill voice that curdled the blood.

"We will not find our own way. You will find our way for us. You will provide us with a Guide."

"Guides are only for officers," the clerk protested weakly, then gasped as a steel-bar finger ground him in the stomach.

"Treat us like officers," the sergeant breathed. "We don't mind."

With chattering teeth the clerk ordered a guide, and a small metal door in the far wall crashed open. The Guide had a tubular metal body that ran on six rubber-tired wheels, a head fashioned to resemble a hound dog's, and a springy metal tail. "Here, boy," the sergeant commanded, and the Guide rushed over to him, slipped out a red plastic tongue, and, with a slight grinding of gears, began to emit the sound of mechanical panting. The sergeant took the length of printed tape and quickly punched the code 1457-D K9 823-7 492 FLM 34 62 on the buttons that decorated the Guide's head. There were two sharp barks, the red tongue vanished, the tail vibrated, and the Guide rolled away down the corridor. The veterans followed.

It took them an hour, by slideway, escalator, elevator, pneumocar, shanks' mare, monorail, moving sidewalk, and greased pole to reach room 62. While they were seated on the slideway they secured the chains of their floor plans to their belts, since even Bill was beginning to realize the value of a guide to this world-sized city. At the door to room 62 the Guide barked three times, then rolled away before they could grab it.

"Should have been quicker," the sergeant said. "Those things are worth their weight in diamonds." He pushed the door open to reveal a fat man seated at a desk shouting into a visisphone.

"I don't give a flying bowb what your excuses are, excuses I can buy wholesale. All I know is I got a production sched-ule and the cameras are ready to roll and where are my prin-

77

cipals? I ask you—and what do you tell me—" he looked up and began to scream, "Out! Out! Can't you see I'm busy!"

The sergeant reached over and threw the visisphone onto the floor then stomped it to tiny smoking bits.

"You have a direct way of getting attention," Bill said.

"Two years in combat make you very direct," the sergeant said, and grated his teeth together in a loud and disturbing way. Then, "Here we are, Ratt, what do we do?"

Producer Ratt kicked his way through the wreckage and threw open a door behind the desk. "Places! Lights!" he shrieked, and there was an immense scurrying and a sudden glare. The to-be-honored veterans followed him through the door into an immense sound stage humming with organized bustle. Cameras on motorized dollies rolled around the set where flats and props simulated the end of a regal throne room. The stained-glass windows glowed with imaginary sunlight, and a golden sunbeam from a spotlight illuminated the throne. Goaded on by the director's screamed instructions the crowd of nobility and high-ranking officers took positions before the throne.

"He called them bowbs!" Bill gasped. "He'll be shot!"

"Are you ever stupid," the gunner said, unreeling a length of flex from his right leg and plugging it into an outlet to recharge his batteries. "Those are all actors. You think they can get real nobility for a thing like this?"

"We only got time to run through this once before the Emperor gets here, so no mistakes." Director Ratt clambered up and settled himself on the throne. "I'll stand in for the Emp. Now you principals, you got the easiest roles, and I don't want you to flub it. We got no time for retakes. You get into position there, that's the stuff, in a row, and when I say *roll* you snap to attention like you been taught or the taxpayers been wasting their money. You there, the guy on the left that's built into the bird cage, keep your damn

78

motors turned off, you're lousing up the soundtrack. Grind gears once more and I'll pull all your fuses. Affirm. You just stay at attention until your name is called, take one pace forward, and snap into a brace. The Emperor will pin a medal on you, salute, drop the salute, and take one pace back. You got that, or is it too complicated for your tiny, indoctrinated minds?"

"Why don't you blow it out!" the sergeant snarled.

"Very witty. All right—let's run through it!"

They rehearsed the ceremony twice before there was a tremendous braying of bugles, and six generals with death-ray pistols at the ready double-timed onto the set and halted with their backs to the throne. All of the extras, cameramen, and technicians—even Director Ratt—bowed low while the veterans snapped to attention. The Emperor shuffled in, climbed the dais, and dropped into the throne. "Continue . . ." he said in a bored voice, and belched lightly behind his hand.

"Let's ROLL!" the director howled at the top of his lungs, and staggered out of camera range. Music rose up in a mighty wave, and the ceremony began. While the Awards and Protocol officer read off the nature of the heroic deeds the noble heroes had accomplished to win that noblest of all medals, the Purple Dart with Coalsack Nebula Cluster, the Emperor rose from his throne and strode majestically forward. The infantry sergeant was first, and Bill watched out of the corner of his eye while the Emperor took an ornate gold, silver, ruby, and platinum medal from the proferred case and pinned it to the man's chest. Then the sergeant stepped back into position, and it was Bill's turn. As from an immense distance he heard his name spoken in rolling tones of thunder, and he strode forward with every ounce of precision that he had been taught back at Camp Leon Trotsky. There, just before him, was the most beloved man in the galaxy! The long and swollen nose that graced a billion banknotes was pointed toward him. The overshot jaw and protruding teeth that filled a billion TV screens was speaking his name. One of the imperial strabismic eyes was pointing at *him!* Passion welled in Bill's bosom like great breakers thundering onto a shore. He snapped his snappiest salute.

In fact he snapped just about the snappiest salute possible, since there aren't very many people with two right arms. Both arms swung up in precise circles, both elbows quivered at right angles, both palms clicked neatly against both eyebrows. It was well done and took the Emperor by surprise, and for one vibrating instant he managed to get both eyeballs pointed at Bill at the same time before they wandered away at random again. The Emperor, still a little disturbed by the unusual salute, groped for the medal and plunged the pin through Bill's tunic squarely into his shivering flesh.

Bill felt no pain, but the sudden stab triggered the growing emotion that had been rushing through him. Dropping the salutes he fell to his knees in good old peasant-serf style, just like a historical TV, which in fact was just where his obsequious subconscious had dredged up the idea from, and seized the Emperor's knob-knuckled and liver-spotted hand. "Father to us all!" Bill exulted, and kissed the hand.

Grim-eyed, the bodyguard of generals leaped forward, and death beat sable wings over Bill, but the Emperor smiled as he pulled his hand gently away and wiped the saliva off on Bill's tunic. A casual flick of his finger restored the bodyguard to position, and he moved on to the gunner, pinned on the remaining medal, and stepped back.

"Cut!" Director Ratt shouted. "Print that, it's a natural with that dumb hick going through the slobbering act."

As Bill struggled back to his feet he saw that the Emperor had not returned to the throne but was instead standing in the midst of the milling crowd of actors. The bodyguard had vanished. Bill blinked, bewildered, as a man whipped the Emperor's crown from his head, popped it into a box, and hurried away with it.

"The brake is jammed," the gunner said, still saluting with a vibrating arm. "Pull the damn thing down for me. It never works right above shoulder level."

"But—the Emperor—" Bill said, tugging at the locked arm until the brakes squealed and released.

"An actor—what else? Do you think they have the *real* Emperor giving out medals to other-ranks? Field grade and higher, I bet. But they put on a bit of an act with him so some poor rube, like you, can get carried away. You were great."

"Here you are," a man said, handing them both stamped metal copies of the medals they were wearing and whipping off the originals.

"Places!" the director's amplified voice boomed. "We got just ten minutes to run through the Empress and the baby kissing with the Aldebranian septuplets for the Fertility Hour. Get those plastic babies out here, and get those damn spectators off the set."

The heroes were pushed into the corridor and the door slammed and locked behind them.

II

"I'm tired," the gunner said, "and besides, my burns hurt." He had had a short circuit during action in the Enlisted Men's Olde Knocking Shoppe and had set the bed on fire.

"Aw, come on," Bill insisted. "We have three-day passes before our ship leaves, and we are on Helior, the Imperial Planet! What riches there are to see here, the Hanging Gardens, the Rainbow Fountains, the Jeweled Palaces. You can't miss them."

"Just watch me. As soon as I catch up on some sleep it's back to the Olde Knocking Shoppe for me. If you're so hot on someone holding your hand while you go sightseeing, take the sergeant."

"He's still drunk."

The infantry sergeant was a solitary drinker who did not believe in cutting corners. Neither did he believe in dilution or in wasting money on fancy packaging. He had used all of his money to bribe a medical orderly and had obtained two carboys of 99 per cent pure grain alcohol, a drum of glucose and saline solution, a hypodermic needle, and a length of rubber tubing. The ethyl-glucose-saline mixture in carboys had been slung from a rafter over his bunk with the tubing leading to the needle plunged into his arm and taped into place as an intravenous drip. Now he was unmoving, well fed, and completely blind-drunk all the time, and if the metered flow were undisturbed he should stay drunk for two and a half years.

Bill put a finishing gloss on his boots and locked the brush into his locker with the rest of his gear. He might be late getting back: it was easy to get lost here on Helior when you didn't have a Guide. It had taken them almost an entire day to find their way from the studio to their quarters even with the sergeant, a man who knew all about maps, leading the way. As long as they stayed near their own area there was no problem, but Bill had had his fill of the homely pleasures provided for the fighting men. He wanted to see Helior, the real Helior, the first city of the galaxy. If no one would go with him, he would do it alone.

It was very hard, in spite of the floor plan, to tell just exactly how far away anything was on Helior, since the diagrams were all diagrammatic and had no scale. But the trip he was planning seemed to be a long one, since one of the key bits of transportation, an evacuated tunnellinear magnetic car, went across at least eighty-four submaps. His destination might very well be on the other side of the planet! A city as large as a planet! The concept was almost too big to grasp! In fact, when he thought about it, the concept *was* too big to grasp.

The sandwiches he had bought from the dispenser in the barracks ran out before he was halfway to his destination, and his stomach, greedily getting adjusted to solid food again, rumbled complaints until he left the slideway in Area 9266-L, Level something or other, or wherever the hell he was, and looked for a canteen. He was obviously in a Typing Area, because the crowds were composed almost completely of women with rounded shoulders and great, long fingers. The only canteen he could find was jammed with them, and he sat in the middle of the high-pitched, yattering crowd and forced himself to eat a meal composed of the only available food: dated-fruitbread-cheese-and-anchovy-paste sandwiches and mashed potatoes with raisin and onion sauce, washed down by herb tea served lukewarm in cups the size of his thumb. It wouldn't have been so bad if the dispenser hadn't automatically covered everything with butterscotch sauce. None of the girls seemed to notice him, since they were all under light hypnosis during the working day in order to cut down their error percentages. He worked his way through the food feeling very much like a ghost as they tittered and yammered over and around him, their fingers, if they weren't eating, compulsively typing their words onto the edge of the table while they talked. He finally escaped, but the meal had had a depressing effect, and this was probably where he made the mistake and boarded the wrong car.

Since the same level and block numbers were repeated in every area, it was possible to get into the wrong area and spend a good deal of time getting good and lost before the mistake was finally realized. Bill did this, and after the usual astronomical number of changes and varieties of transportation he boarded the elevator that terminated, he thought, in the galaxy-famed Palace Gardens. All of the other passengers got off on lower levels, and the robelevator picked up speed as it hurtled up to the topmost level. He rose into the air as it braked to a stop, and his ears popped with the pressure change, and when the doors opened he stepped out into a snow-filled wind. He gaped about with unbelief and behind him the doors snicked shut and the elevator vanished.

The doors had opened directly onto the metal plain that made up the topmost layer of the city, now obscured by the swirling clouds of snow. Bill groped for the button to recall the elevator, when a vagrant swirl of wind whipped the snow away and the warm sun beat down on him from the cloudless sky. This was impossible.

"This is impossible," Bill said with forthright indignation.

"Nothing is impossible if I will it," a scratchy voice spoke from behind Bill's shoulder. "For I am the Spirit of Life."

Bill skittered sideways like a homeostatic robhorse, rolling his eyes at the small, white-whiskered man with a twitching nose and red-rimmed eyes who had appeared soundlessly behind him.

"You got a leak in your think-tank," Bill snapped, angry at himself for being so goosy.

"You'd be nuts, too, on this job," the little man sobbed, and knuckled a pendant drop from his nose. "Half-froze, half-cooked and half-wiped out most of the time on oxy. The Spirit of Life," he quavered, "mine is the power . . ."

"Now that you mention it," Bill's words were muffled by a sudden flurry of snow, "I am feeling a bit high myself. Wheeee . . . !!" The wind veered and swept the occluding clouds of snow away, and Bill gaped at the suddenly revealed view.

Slushy snow and pools of water spotted the surface as far as he could see. The golden coating had been worn away, and the metal was gray and pitted beneath, streaked with ruddy rivulets of rust. Rows of great pipes, each thicker than a man is tall, snaked toward him from over the horizon and ended in funnel-like mouths. The funnels were obscured by whirling clouds of vapor and snow that shot high into the air with a hushed roar, though one of the vapor columns collapsed and the cloud dispersed while Bill watched.

"Number eighteen blown!" the old man shouted into a microphone, grabbed a clipboard from the wall, and kicked his way through the slush toward a rusty and dilapidated walkway that groaned and rattled along parallel with the pipes. Bill followed, shouting at the man, who now completely ignored him. As the walkway, clanking and swaying, carried them along, Bill began to wonder just where the pipes led, and after a minute, when his head cleared a bit, curiosity got the better of him and he strained ahead to see what the mysterious bumps were on the horizon. They slowly resolved themselves into a row of giant spaceships, each one connected to one of the thick pipes. With unexpected agility the old man sprang from the walkway and bounded toward the ship at station eighteen, where the tiny figures of workers, high up, were disconnecting the seals that joined the ship to the pipe. The old man copied numbers from a meter attached to the pipe, while Bill watched a crane swing over with the end of a large, flexible hose that emerged from the surface they were standing on. It was attached to the valve on top of the spaceship. A rumbling vibration shook the hose, and from around the seal to the ship emerged puffs of black cloud that drifted over the stained metal plain.

"Could I ask just what the hell is going on here?" Bill said plaintively.

"Life! Life everlasting!" the old man crowed, swinging up from the glooms of his depression toward the heights of manic elation.

"Could you be a little more specific?"

"Here is a world sheathed in metal," he stamped his foot and there was a dull boom. "What does that mean?"

"It means the world is sheathed in metal."

"Correct. For a trooper you show a remarkable turn of intelligence. So you take a planet and cover it with metal, and you got a planet where the only green growing things are in the Imperial Gardens and a couple of window boxes. Then what do you have?"

"Everybody dead," Bill said, for after all, he was a farm boy and up on all the photosynthesis and chlorophyll bowb.

"Correct again. You and I and the Emperor and a couple of billion other slobs are working away turning all the oxygen into carbon dioxide, and with no plants around to turn it back into oxygen and if we keep at it long enough we breathe ourselves to death."

"Then these ships are bringing in liquid oxygen?"

The old man bobbed his head and jumped back onto the slideway; Bill followed. "Affirm. They get it for free on the agricultural planets. And after they empty here they load up with carbon extracted at great expense from the CO_2 and whip back with it to the hickworlds, where it is burned for fuel, used for fertilizer, combined into numberless plastics and other products . . ."

Bill stepped from the slideway at the nearest elevator, while the old man and his voice vanished into the vapor, and crouching down, his head pounding from the oxy jag, he began flipping furiously through his floor plan. While he waited for the elevator he found his place from the code number on the door and began to plot a new course toward the Palace Gardens.

This time he did not allow himself to be distracted. By only eating candy bars and drinking carbonated beverages from the dispensers along his route he avoided the dangers and distractions of the eateries, and by keeping himself awake he avoided missing connections. With black bags under his eyes and teeth rotting in his head he stumbled from a grav-shaft and with thudding heart finally saw a florally decorated and colorfully illuminated scentsign that said HANGING GAR-DENS. There was an entrance turnstile and a cashier's window.

"One please."

"That'll be ten imperial bucks."

"Isn't that a little expensive?" he said peevishly, unrolling the bills one by one from his thin wad.

"If you're poor, don't come to Helior."

The cashier-robot was primed with all the snappy answers. Bill ignored it and pushed through into the gardens. They were everything he had ever dreamed of and more. As he walked down the gray cinder path inside the outer wall he could see green shrubs and grass just on the other side of the titanium mesh fence. No more than a hundred yards away, on the other side of the grass, were floating, colorful plants and flowers from all the worlds of the Empire. And there! Tiny in the distance were the Rainbow Fountains, almost visible to the naked eye. Bill slipped a coin into one of the telescopes and watched their colors glow and wane, and it was just as good as seeing it on TV. He went on, circling inside the wall, bathed by the light of the artificial sun in the giant dome above.

But even the heady pleasures of the gardens waned in the face of the soul-consuming fatigue that gripped him in iron hands. There were steel benches pegged to the wall, and he dropped onto one to rest for a moment, then closed his eyes for a second to ease the glare. His chin dropped onto his chest, and before he realized it he was sound asleep. Other visitors scrunched by on the cinders without disturbing him, nor did he move when one sat down at the far end of the bench.

Since Bill never saw this man there is no point in describing him. Suffice to say that he had sallow skin, a broken, reddened nose, feral eyes peering from under a simian brow, wide hips and narrow shoulders, mismatched feet, lean, knobby, dirty fingers, and a twitch.

Long seconds of eternity ticked by while the man sat there. Then for a few moments there were no other visitors in sight. With a quick, snakelike motion the newcomer whipped an atomic arc-pencil from his pocket. The small, incredibly hot flame whispered briefly as he pressed it against the chain that secured Bill's floor plan to his waist, just at the point where the looped chain rested on the metal bench. In a trice the metal of the chain was welded fast to the metal of the bench. Still undisturbed, Bill slept on.

A wolfish grin flickered across the man's face like the evil rings formed in sewer water by a diving rat. Then, with a single swift motion, the atomic flame severed the chain near the volume. Pocketing the arc-pencil the thief rose, plucked Bill's floor plan from his lap, and strode quickly away.

III

At first Bill didn't appreciate the magnitude of his loss. He swam slowly up out of his sleep, thickheaded, with the feeling that something was wrong. Only after repeated tugging did he realize that the chain was stuck fast to the bench and that the book was gone. The chain could not be freed, and in the end he had to unfasten it from his belt and leave it dangling. Retracing his steps to the entrance, he knocked on the cashier's window.

"No refunds," the robot said.

"I want to report a crime."

"The police handle crime. You want to talk to the police. You talk to the police on a phone. Here is a phone. The number is 111-11-111." A small door slid open, and a phone popped out, catching Bill in the chest and knocking him back on his heels. He dialed the number.

"Police," a voice said, and a bulldog-faced sergeant wearing a Prussian blue uniform and a scowl appeared on the screen.

"I want to report a theft."

"Grand larceny or petty larceny?"

"I don't know, it was my floor plan that was stolen."

"Petty larceny. Proceed to your nearest police station. This is an emergency circuit, and you are tying it up illegally. The penalty for illegally tying up an emergency circuit is . . ." Bill jammed hard on the button and the screen went blank. He turned back to the robot cashier.

"No refunds," it said. Bill snarled impatiently.

"Shut up. All I want to know is where the nearest police station is."

"I am a cashier robot, not an information robot. That information is not in my memory. I suggest you consult your floor plan."

"But it's my floor plan that has been stolen!"

"I suggest you talk to the police."

"But . . ." Bill turned red and kicked the cashier's box angrily. "No refunds," it said as he stalked away.

"Drinky, drinky, make you stinky," a robot bar said, rolling up and whispering in his ear. It made the sound of ice cubes rattling in a frosty glass.

"A damn good idea. Beer. A large one." He pushed coins into its money slot and clutched at the dispos-a-stein that rattled down the chute and almost bounced to the ground. It cooled and refreshed him and calmed his anger. He looked at the sign that said To THE JEWELED PALACE. "I'll go to the palace, have a look-see, then find someone there who can direct me to the police station. Ouch!" The robot bar had pulled the dispos-a-stein from his hand, almost taking his forefinger with it, and with unerring robotic aim hurled it thirty-two feet into the open mouth of a rubbish shaft that projected from a wall.

The Jeweled Palace appeared to be about as accessible as the Hanging Gardens, and he decided to report the theft before paying his way into the grilled enclosure that circled the palace at an awesome distance. There was a policeman hanging out his belly and idly spinning his club near the entrance who should know where the police station was.

"Where's the police station?" Bill asked.

"I ain't no information booth—use your floor plan."

"But"—through teeth tightly clamped together—"I cannot. My floor plan has been stolen and that is why I want to find Yipe!"

Bill said Yipe! because the policeman, with a practiced motion, had jammed the end of his club up into Bill's armpit and pushed him around the corner with it.

"I used to be a trooper myself before I bought my way out," the officer said.

"I would enjoy your reminiscences more if you took the club out of my armpit," Bill moaned, then sighed gratefully as the club vanished.

"Since I used to be a trooper I don't want to see a buddy with the Purple Dart with Coalsack Nebula Cluster get into trouble. I am also an honest cop and don't take bribes, but if a buddy was to loan me twenty-five bucks until payday I would be much obliged."

Bill had been born stupid, but he was learning. The money appeared and vanished swiftly, and the cop relaxed, clacking the end of his club against his yellow teeth.

"Let me tell you something, pal, before you make any official statements to me in my official capacity, since up to now we have just been talking buddy-buddy. There are a lot of ways to get into trouble here on Helior, but the easiest is to lose your floor plan. It is a hanging offense on Helior. I know a guy what went into the station to report that someone got his plan and they slapped the cuffs on him inside ten seconds, maybe five. Now what was it you wanted to say to me?"

"You got a match?"

"I don't smoke."

"Good-by."

"Take it easy, pal."

Bill scuttled around another corner and leaned against the wall breathing deeply. Now what? He could barely find his way around this place with the plan—how could he do it without one? There was a leaden weight pulling at his insides that he tried to ignore. He forced away the feeling of terror and tried to think. But thinking made him lightheaded. It seemed like years since he had had a good meal, and thinking of food he began to pump saliva at such a great rate that he almost drowned. Food, that's what he needed, food for thought; he had to relax over a nice, juicy steak, and when the inner man was satisfied he would be able to think clearly and find a way out of this mess. There must be a way out. He had almost a full day left before he was due back from leave; there was plenty of time. Staggering around a sharp bend he came out into a high tunnel brilliant with lights, the most brilliant of which was a sign that said THE GOLD SPACE SUIT.

"The Gold Space Suit," Bill said. "That's more like it. Galaxy-famous on countless TV programs, what a restaurant, that's the way to build up the old morale. It'll be expensive, but what the hell . . ."

Tightening his belt and straightening his collar, he strode up the wide gold steps and through the imitation spacelock. The headwaiter beckoned him and smiled, soft music wafted his way and the floor opened beneath his feet. Scratching helplessly at the smooth walls, he shot down the golden tube which turned gradually until, when he emerged, he shot through the air and fell, sprawling, into a dusty metal alley-way. Ahead of him, painted on the wall with foot-high letters, was the imperious message, GET LOST BUM.

He stood and dusted himself, and a robot sidled over and crooned in his ear with the voice of a young and lovely girl, "I bet you're hungry, darling. Why not try Giuseppe Singh's neo-Indian curried pizza? You're just a few steps from Singh's, directions are on the back of the card."

The robot took a card from a slot in its chest and put it carefully into Bill's mouth. It was a cheap and badly adjusted robot. Bill spluttered the soggy card out and wiped it on his handkerchief.

"What happened?" he asked.

"I bet you're hungry, darling, grrrr-ark." The robot switched to another recorded message, cued by Bill's question. "You have just been ejected from The Gold Space Suit, galaxy-famous on countless TV programs, because you are a cheap bum. When you entered this establishment you were X-rayed and the contents of your pockets automatically computed. Since the contents of your pockets obviously fell below the minimum with cover charge, one drink, and tax, you were ejected. But you are still hungry, aren't you darling?" The robot leered, and the dulcet, sexy voice poured from between the broken gaps of its mouthplate. "C'mon down to Singh's where food is good and cheap. Try Singh's yummy lasagna with dhal and lime sauce."

Bill went, not because he wanted some loathsome Bombay-Italian concoction, but because of the map and instructions on the back of the card. There was a feeling of security in knowing he was going from somewhere to somewhere again, following the directions, clattering down this stair well, dropping in that gravchute, grabbing for a place in the right hookway. After one last turning his nose was assaulted by a wave of stale fat, old garlic, and charred flesh, and he knew he was there.

The food was incredibly expensive and far worse than he had ever imagined it could be, but it stilled the painful rumbling in his stomach, by direct assault if not by pleasant satiation. With one fingernail he attempted to pry horrible pieces of gristle from between his teeth while he looked at the man across the table from him, who was moaning as he forced down spoonfuls of something nameless. His tablemate was dressed in colorful holiday clothes and looked a fat, ruddy, and cheerful type.

"Hi . . . !" Bill said, smiling.

"Go drop dead," the man snarled.

"All I said was Hi." Petulantly.

"That's enough. Everyone who has bothered to talk to me in the sixteen hours I been on this so-called pleasure planet has cheated or screwed me or stolen my money one way or another. I am next to broke and I still have six days left of my See Helior and Live tour."

"I only wanted to ask you if I could sort of look through your floor plan while you were eating."

"I told you, everyone is out to screw me out of something. Drop dead."

"Please."

"I'll do it—for twenty-five bucks, cash in advance, and only as long as I'm eating."

"Done!" Bill slapped the money down, whipped under the table, and, sitting cross-legged, began to flip furiously through the volume, writing down travel instructions as fast as he could plot a course. Above him the fat man continued to eat and groan, and whenever he hit a particularly bad mouthful he would jerk the chain and make Bill lose his place. Bill had charted a route almost halfway to the haven of the Transit Ranker's Center before the man pulled the book away and stamped out.

When Odysseus returned from his terror-haunted voyage he spared Penelope's ears the incredible details of his journey. When Richard Lion-Heart, freed finally from his dungeon, came home from the danger-filled years of the Crusades, he did not assault Queen Berengaria's sensibilities with horror-full anecdotes; he simply greeted her and unlocked her chastity belt. Neither will I, gentle reader, profane your hearing with the dangers and despairs of Bill's journeyings, for they are beyond imagining. Suffice to say he did it. He reached the T.R.C.

Through red-rimmed eyes he blinked at the sign, Transit Rankers' Center it said, then had to lean against the wall as relief made his knees weak. He had done it! He had only overstayed his leave by eight days, and that couldn't matter too much. Soon now he would be back in the friendly arms of the troopers again, away from the endless miles of metal corridors, the constantly rushing crowds, the slipways, slide-ways, gravdrops, hellavators, suctionlifts, and all the rest. He would get stinking drunk with his buddies and let the alcohol dissolve the memories of his terrible travels, try to forget the endless horror of those days of wandering without food or water or sound of human voice, endlessly stumbling through the Stygian stacks in the Carbon Paper Levels. It was all behind him now. He dusted his scruffy uniform, shamefully aware of the rips, crumplings, and missing buttons that de-faced it. If he could get into the barracks without being stopped he would change uniforms before reporting to the orderly room.

A few heads turned his way, but he made it all right through the day room and into the barracks. Only his mattress was rolled up, his blankets were gone and his locker empty. It was beginning to look as though he was in trouble, and trouble in the troopers is never a simple thing. Repressing a cold feeling of despair he washed up a bit in the latrine, took a stiffening drink from the cold tap, then dragged his feet to the orderly room. The first sergeant was at his desk, a giant, powerful, sadistic-looking man with dark skin the same color as that of his old buddy Tembo. He held a plastic doll dressed in a captain's uniform in one hand, and was pushing straightened-out paper clips into it with the other. Without turning his head he rolled his eyes toward Bill and scowled.

"You're in bad trouble, trooper, coming into the orderly room out of uniform like that."

"I'm in worse trouble than you think, Sarge," Bill said lean-ing weakly on the desk. The sergeant stared at Bill's mis-matched hands, his eyes flickering back and forth quickly from one to the other.

"Where did you get that hand, trooper? Speak up! I know that hand."

"It belonged to a buddy of mine, and I have the arm that goes with it too."

Anxious to get onto any subject other than his military crimes, Bill held the hand out for the sergeant to look at. But he was horrified when the fingers tensed into a rock-hard fist, the muscles bunched on his arm and the fist flew forward to catch the first sergeant square on the jaw and knocked him backward off his chair ass over applecart. "Sergeant!" Bill screamed, and grabbed the rebellious hand with his other and forced it, not without a struggle, back to his side.

The sergeant rose slowly, and Bill backed away, shuddering. He could not believe it when the sergeant reseated himself and Bill saw that he saw smiling.

"Thought I knew that hand, belongs to my old buddy Tembo. We always joked like that. You take good care of that arm, you hear? Is there any more of Tembo around?" and when Bill said no, he knocked out a quick tom-tom beat on the edge of the desk. "Well, he's gone to the Big Ju-ju Rite in the Sky." The smile vanished and the snarl reappeared. "You're in bad trouble, trooper. Let's see your ID card."

He whipped it from Bill's nerveless fingers and shoved it into a slot in the desk. Lights flickered, the mechanism hummed and vibrated and a screen lit up. The first sergeant read the message there, and as he did the snarl faded from his face and was replaced by an expression of cold anger. When he turned back to Bill his eyes were narrowed slits that pinned him with a gaze that could curdle milk in an instant or destroy minor life forms like rodents or cockroaches. It chilled Bill's blood in his veins and sent a shiver through his body that made it sway like a tree in the wind.

"Where did you steal this ID card? Who are you?"

On the third try Bill managed to force words between his

paralyzed lips. "It's me . . . that's my card . . . I'm me, Fuse Tender First Class Bill . . ."

"You are a liar." A fingernail uniquely designed for ripping out jugular veins flicked at the card. "This card must be stolen, because First Class Fuse Tender Bil shipped out of here eight days ago. That is what the record says, and records do not lie. You've had it, Bowb." He depressed a red button labeled MILITARY POLICE, and an alarm bell could be heard ringing angrily in the distance. Bill shuffled his feet, and his eyes rolled, searching for some way to escape. "Hold him there, Tembo," the sergeant snapped, "I want to get to the bottom of this."

Bill's left-right arm grabbed the edge of the desk, and he couldn't pry it lose. He was still struggling with it when heavy boots thudded up behind him.

"What's up?" a familiar voice growled.

"Impersonation of a non-commissioned officer plus lesser charges that don't matter because the first charge alone calls for electro-arc lobectomy and thirty lashes."

"Oh, sir," Bill laughed, spinning about and feasting his eyes on a long-loathed figure. "Deathwish Drang! Tell them you know me."

One of the two men was the usual red-hatted, clubbed, gunned, and polished brute in human form. But the other one could only be Deathwish.

"Do you know the prisoner?" the first sergeant asked.

Deathwish squinted, rolling his eyes the length of Bill's body. "I knew a Sixth-class fuse-fingerer named Bill, but both his hands matched. Something very strange here. We'll rough him up a bit in the guardhouse and let you know what he confesses."

"Affirm. But watch out for that left hand. It belongs to a friend of mine."

"Won't lay a finger on it."

"But I am Bill!" Bill shouted. "That's me, my card, I can prove it."

"An imposter," the sergeant said, and pointed to the controls on his desk. "The records say that First Class Fuse Tender Bil shipped out of here eight days ago. And records don't lie."

"Records *can't* lie, or there would be no order in the universe," Deathwish said, grinding his club deep into Bill's gut and shoving him toward the door. "Did those back-ordered thumbscrews come in yet?" he asked the other MP.

It could only have been fatigue that caused Bill to do what he did then. Fatigue, desperation, and fear combined and overpowered him, for at heart he was a good trooper and had learned to be Brave and Clean and Reverent and Heterosexual and all the rest. But every man has his breaking point, and Bill had reached his. He had faith in the impartial working of justice—never having learned any better—but it was the thought of torture that bugged him. When his fear-crazed eyes saw the sign on the wall that read LAUNDRY, a synapse closed without conscious awareness on his part, and he leaped forward, his sudden desperate action breaking the grip on his arm. Escape! Behind that flap on the wall must lie a laundry chute with a pile of nice soft sheets and towels at the bottom that would ease his fall. He could get away! Ignoring the harsh, beastlike cries of the MPs, he dived headfirst through the opening.

He fell about four feet, landed headfirst, and almost brained himself. There was not a chute here but a deep, strong metal laundry basket.

Behind him the MPs beat at the swinging flap, but they could not budge it, since Bill's legs had jammed up behind it and stopped it from swinging open.

"It's locked!" Deathwish cried. "We've been had! Where

does this laundry chute go?" Making the same mistaken assumption as Bill.

"I don't know, I'm a new man here myself," the other man gasped.

"You'll be new man in the electric chair if we don't find that bowb!"

The voices dimmed as the heavy boots thudded away, and Bill stirred. His neck was twisted at an odd angle and hurt, his knees crunched into his chest, and he was half suffocated by the cloth jammed into his face. He tried to straighten his legs and pushed against the metal wall; there was a click as something snapped, and he fell forward as the laundry basket dropped out into the serviceway on the other side of the wall.

"There he is!" a familiarly hateful voice shouted, and Bill staggered away. The running boots were just behind him when he came to the gravchute and once more dived headfirst, with considerably greater success this time. As the apoplectic MPs sprang in after him the automatic cycling circuit spaced them all out a good fifteen feet apart. It was a slow, drifting fall, and Bill's vision finally cleared and he looked up and shuddered at the sight of Deathwish's fang-filled physiognomy drifting down behind him.

"Old buddy," Bill sobbed, clasping his hands prayerfully. "Why are you chasing me?"

"Don't buddy me, you Chinger spy. You're not even a good spy—your arms don't match." As he dropped Deathwish pulled his gun free of the holster and aimed it squarely between Bill's eyes. "Shot while attempting to escape."

"Have mercy!" Bill pleaded.

"Death to all Chingers." He pulled the trigger.

IV

The bullet plowed slowly out of the cloud of expanding gas and drifted about two feet toward Bill before the humming gravity field slowed it to a stop. The simple-minded cycling circuit translated the bullet's speed as mass and assumed that another body had entered the gravchute and assigned it a position. Deathwish's fall slowed until he was fifteen feet behind the bullet, while the other MP also assumed the same relative position behind him. The gap between Bill and his pursuers was now twice as wide, and he took advantage of this and ducked out of the exit at the next level. An open elevator beckoned to him coyly and he was into it and had the door closed before the wildly cursing Deathwish could emerge from the shaft.

After this, escape was simply a matter of muddling his trail. He used different means of transportation at random, and all the time kept fleeing to lower levels as though seeking to escape like a mole by burrowing deep into the ground. It was exhaustion that stopped him finally, dropping him in his tracks, slumped against a wall and panting like a triceratops in heat. Gradually he became aware of his surroundings and realized that he had come lower than he had ever been before. The corridors were gloomier and older, made of steel plates riveted together. Massive pillars, some a hundred feet or more in diameter, broke the smoothness of the walls, great structures that supported the mass of the world-city above. Most of the doors he saw were locked and bolted, hung with elaborate seals. It was darker, too, he realized, as he wearily dragged to his feet and went looking for something to drink: his throat burned like fire. A drink dispenser was let into the wall ahead and was different from most of the ones he was used to in that it had thick steel bars reinforcing the front of the mechanism and was adorned with a large sign that read THIS MACHINE PROTECTED BY YOU-COOK-EM BURGLAR ALARMS— ANY ATTEMPT TO BREAK INTO THE MECHANISM WILL RE- LEASE 100,000 VOLTS THROUGH THE CULPRIT RESPONSIBLE. He found enough coins in his pocket to buy a double Heroin- Cola and stepped carefully back out of the range of any sparks while the cup filled.

He felt much better after draining it, until he looked in his wallet then he felt much worse. He had eight imperial bucks to his name, and when they were gone—then what? Self-pity broke through his exhausted and drug-ridden senses, and he wept. He was vaguely aware of occasional passersby but paid them no heed. Not until three men stopped close by and let a fourth sink to the floor. Bill glanced at them, then looked away; their words coming dimly to his ears made no sense, since he was having a far better time wallowing in lacrimose indulgence.

"Poor old Golph, looks like he's done for."

"That's for sure. He's rattling just about the nicest death rattle I ever heard. Leave him here for the cleaning robots."

"But what about the *job?* We need four to pull it."

"Let's take a look at deplanned over there."

A heavy boot in Bill's side rolled him over and caught his attention. He blinked up at the circle of men all similar in their tattered clothes, dirty skins, and bearded faces. They were different in size and shape, though they all had one thing in common. None of them carried a floor plan, and they all looked strangely naked without the heavy, pendant volumes.

"Where's your floor plan?" the biggest and hairiest asked, and kicked Bill again.

"Stolen . . ." he started to sob again.

"Are you a trooper?"

"They took away my ID card . . ."

"Got any bucks?"

"Gone . . . all gone . . . like the dispos-a-steins of yester-year . . ."

"Then you are one of the deplanned," the watchers chanted in unison, and helped Bill to his feet. "Now—join with us in 'The Song of the Deplanned,'" and with quavering voices they sang:

> Stand together one and all,
> For Brothers Deplanned always shall,
> Unite and fight to achieve the Right,
> That Might shall fail and Truth avail,
> So that we, who once were free, can someday be
> Once more free to see the skies of blue above,
> And hear the gentle pitty-pat
> Of snow.

"It doesn't rhyme very well," Bill said.

"Ah, we's short of talent down here, we is," the smallest and oldest deplanned said, and coughed a hacking, rachitic cough.

"Shut up," the big one said, and kidney-punched the old one and Bill. "I'm Litvok, and this is my bunch. You part of my bunch now, newcomer, and your name is Golph 28169-minus."

"No, I'm not; my name is Bill, and it's easier to say—" He was slugged again.

"Shaddup! Bill's a hard name because it's a new name, and I never remember no new names. I always got a Golph 28169-minus in my bunch. What's your name?"

"Bill— OUCH! I mean Golph!"

"That's better—but don't forget you got a last name too . . ."

"I is hungry," the old one whined. "When we gonna make the raid?"

"Now. Follow me."

They stepped over the old Golph etc. who had expired while the new one was being initiated, and hurried away down a dark, dank back passage. Bill followed along, wondering what he had got himself into, but too weary to worry about it now. They were talking about food; after he had some food he would think about what to do next, but meanwhile he felt glad that someone was taking care of him and doing his thinking for him. It was just like being back in the troopers, only better, since you didn't even have to shave.

The little band of men emerged into a brightly lit hallway, cringing a little in the sudden glare. Litvok waved them to a stop and peered carefully in both directions, then cupped one dirt-grimed hand to his cauliflower ear and listened, frowning with the effort.

"It looks clear. Schmutzig, you stay here and give the alarm if anyone comes, Sporco you go down the hall to the next bend, and you do same thing. You, new Golph, come with me."

The two sentries scrambled off to their duties, while Bill followed Litvok into an alcove containing a locked metal door, which the burly leader opened with a single blow of a metal hammer he took from a place of concealment in his ragged clothes. Inside were a number of pipes of assorted dimensions that rose from the floor and vanished into the ceiling above. There were numbers stenciled onto each pipe, and Litvok pointed to them.

"We gotta find kl-9256-B," he said. "Let's go."

Bill found the pipe quickly. It was about as big around as

his wrist, and he had just called to the bunch leader when a shrill whistle sounded down the hall.

"Outside!" Litvok said, and pushed Bill before him, then closed the door and stood so that his body covered the broken lock. There was a growing rumbling and swishing noise that came down the hall toward them as they cowered in the alcove. Litvok held his hammer behind his back as the noise increased, and a sanitation robot appeared and swiveled its binocular eyestalk toward them.

"Will you kindly move, this robot wishes to clean where you are standing," a recorded voice spoke from the robot in firm tones. It whirled its brushes at them hopefully.

"Get lost," Litvok growled.

"Interference with a sanitation robot during the performance of its duties is a punishable crime, as well as an antisocial act. Have you stopped to consider where you would be if the Sanitation Department wasn't . . ."

"Blabbermouth," Litvok snarled and hit the robot on top of its brain case with the hammer. "WONKITY!!" the robot shrilled, and went reeling down the hall dribbling water incontinently from its nozzles. "Let's finish the job," Litvok said, throwing the door open again. He handed the hammer to Bill, and drawing a hacksaw from a place of concealment in his ragged clothes he attacked the pipe with frenzied strokes. The metal pipe was tough, and within a minute he was running with sweat and starting to tire.

"Take over," he shouted at Bill. "Go as fast as you can, then I take over again." Turn and turn about it took them less than three minutes to saw all the way through the pipe. Litvok slipped the saw back into his clothes and picked up the hammer. "Get ready," he said, spitting on his hands and then taking a mighty swing at the pipe.

Two blows did it; the top part of the severed pipe bent out of alignment with the bottom, and from the opening

104

began to pour an endless stream of linked green frankfurters. Litvok grabbed the end of the chain and threw it over Bill's shoulder, then began to coil loops of the things over his shoulders and arms, higher and higher. They reached the level of Bill's eyes and he could read the white lettering stamped all over their grass-green forms. CHLORA-FILLIES they read, and THERE'S SUNSHINE IN EVERY LINK! and THE EQUINE WURST OF DISTINCTION, and TRY OUR DOBBIN-BURGERS NEXT TIME!

"Enough . . ." Bill groaned, staggering under the weight. Litvok snapped the chain and began twining them over his own shoulders, when the flow of shiny green forms suddenly ceased. He pulled the last links from the pipe and pushed out the door.

"The alarm went, they're onto us. Get out fast before the cops get here!" He whistled shrilly, and the lookouts came running to join them. They fled, Bill stumbling under the weight of the wursts, in a nightmare race through tunnels, down stairs, ladders, and oily tubes, until they reached a dusty, deserted area where the dim lights were few and far between. Litvok pried a manhole up from the floor, and they dropped down one by one, to crawl through a cable and tube tunnel between levels. Schmutzig and Sporco came last to pick up the sausages that fell from Bill's aching back. Finally, through a pried-out grill, they reached their coal-black destination, and Bill collapsed onto the rubble-covered floor. With cries of greed the others stripped Bill of his cargo, and within a minute a fire was crackling in a metal wastebasket and the green redhots were toasting on a rack.

The delicious smell of roasting chlorophyll roused Bill, and he looked around with interest. By the flickering firelight he saw that they were in an immense chamber that vanished into the gloom in all directions. Thick pillars supported the ceiling and the city above, while between them loomed immense piles and heaps of all sizes. The old man, Sporco, walked over to the nearest heap and wrenched something free. When he returned Bill could see that he had sheets of paper that he began to feed one by one into the fire. One of the sheets fell near Bill and he saw, before he stuffed it into the flames, that it was a government form of some kind, yellow with age.

Though Bill had never enjoyed Chlora-fillies, he relished them now. Appetite was the sauce, and the burning paper added a new taste tang. They washed the sausages down with rusty water from a pail kept under a permanent drip from a pipe and feasted like kings. This is the good life, Bill thought, pulling another filly from the fire and blowing on it, good food, good drink, good companions. A free man.

Litvok and the old one were already asleep on beds of crumpled paper when the other man, Schmutzig, sidled over to Bill.

"Have you found my ID card?" he asked in a hoarse whisper, and Bill realized the man was mad. The flames reflected eerily from the cracked lenses of his glasses, and Bill could see that they had silver frames and must have once been very expensive. Around Schmutzig's neck, half hidden by his ragged beard, was the cracked remains of a collar and the torn shard of a once fine cravat.

"No I haven't seen your ID card," Bill said, "in fact I haven't seen mine since the first sergeant took it away from me and forgot to give it back." Bill began to feel sorry for himself again, and the foul frankfurters were sitting like lead in his stomach. Schmutzig ignored his answer, immersed as he was in his own far more interesting monomania.

"I'm an important man, you know, Schmutzig von Dreck is a man to be reckoned with, they'll find out. They think they can get away with this, but they can't. An error they said, just a simple error, the tape in the records section broke, and when they repaired it a little weensy bit got snipped out, and that was the piece with my record on it, and the first I heard about it was when my pay didn't arrive at the end of the month and I went to see them about it and they had never heard of me. But *everyone* has heard of me. Von Dreck is a good old name. I was an echelon manager before I was twenty-two and had a staff of 356 under me in the Staple and Paper Clip Division of the 89th Office Supply Wing. So they couldn't make believe they never heard of me, even if I had left my ID card home in my other suit, and they had no reason clearing everything out of my apartment while I was away just because it was rented to what they said was an imaginary person. I could have proven who I was if I had my ID card . . . have you seen my ID card?"

This is where I came in, Bill thought, then aloud, "That sure sounds rough. I'll tell you what I'll do, I'll help you look for it. I'll go down here and see if I can find it."

Before the softheaded Schmutzig could answer Bill had slipped away between the mountainous stacks of old files, very proud of himself for having outwitted a middle-aged nut. He was feeling pleasantly full and tired and didn't want to be bothered again. What he needed was a good night's rest, then in the morning he would think about this mess, maybe figure a way out of it. Feeling his way along the cluttered aisle he put a long distance between himself and the other deplanned before climbing up on a tottering stack of paper and from that clambering to a still higher one. He sighed with relief, arranged a little pile of paper for a pillow and closed his eyes.

Then the lights came on in rows high up on the ceiling of the warehouse and shrill police whistles sounded from all sides and guttural shouts that set him to shivering with fear.

"Grab that one! Don't let him get away!"

"I got the horse thief!"

"You planless bowbs have stolen your last Chlora-filly! It's the uranium-salt mines on Zana-2 for you!"

Then, "Do we have them all—?" and as Bill lay clutching desperately at the forms, with his heart thudding with fear, the answer finally came.

"Yeah, four of them, we been watching them for a long time, ready to pull them in if they tried anything like this."

"But we only got three here."

"I saw the fourth one earlier, getting carried off stiff as a board by a sanitation robot."

"Affirm, then let's go."

Fear lashed through Bill again. How long before one of the bunch talked, ratted to buy a favor for himself, and told the cops that they had just sworn in a new recruit? He had to get out of here. All the police now seemed to be bunched at the wienie roast, and he had to take a chance. Sliding from the pile as silently as he could, he began to creep in the opposite direction. If there was no exit this way he was trapped—no, mustn't think like that! Behind him whistles shrilled again, and he knew the hunt was on. Adrenalin poured into his bloodstream as he spurted forward, while rich, equine protein added strength to his legs and a decided canter to his gait. Ahead was a door, and he hurled his weight against it; for an instant it stuck—then squealed open on rusty hinges. Heedless of danger, he hurled himself down the spiral staircase, down and down, and out of another door, fleeing wildly, thinking only of escape.

Once more, with the instincts of a hunted animal, he fled downward. He did not notice that the walls here were bolted together at places and streaked with rust, nor did he think it unusual when he had to pry open a jammed wooden door— *wood* on a planet that had not seen a tree in a hundred millenia! The air was danker and foul at times, and his fear-ridden course took him through a stone tunnel where nameless beasts fled before him with the rattle of evil claws. There were long stretches now doomed to eternal darkness where he had to feel his way, running his fingers along the repellent and slimy moss covered walls. Where there were lights they glowed but dimly behind their burdens of spider webs and insect corpses. He splashed through pools of stagnant water until, slowly, the strangeness of his surroundings penetrated, and he blinked about him. Set into the floor beneath his feet was another door, and, still gripped by the reflex of flight, he threw it open, but it led nowhere. Instead it gave access to a bin of some kind of granulated material, not unlike coarse sugar. Though it might just as well be insulation. It could be edible: he bent and picked some up between his fingers and ground it between his teeth. No, not edible, he spat it out, though there was something very familiar about it. Then it hit him.

It was dirt. Earth. Soil. Sand. The stuff that planets were made out of, that *this* planet was made out of, it was the surface of Helior, on which the incredible weight of the world-embracing city rested. He looked up, and in that unspeakable moment was suddenly aware of that weight, all that weight, above his head, pressing down and trying to crush him. Now he was on the bottom, rock bottom, and obsessed by galloping claustrophobia. Giving a weak scream, he stumbled down the hallway until it ended in an immense sealed and bolted door. There was no way out of this. And when he looked at the blackened thickness of the door he decided that he really didn't want to go out that way either. What nameless horrors might lurk behind a portal like this at the bottom of the world?

Then, while he watched, paralyzed, with staring eyes, the door squealed and started to swing open. He turned to run and screamed aloud in terror as *something* grabbed him in an unbreakable grip . . .

V

Not that Bill didn't try to break the grip, but it was hopeless. He wriggled in the skeleton-white claws that clutched him and tried futilely to pry them from his arms, all the time uttering helpless little bleats like a lamb in an eagle's talons. Thrashing ineffectually, he was drawn backward through the mighty portal which swung shut without the agency of human hands.

"Welcome . . ." a sepulchral voice said, and Bill staggered as the restraining grasp was removed, then whirled about to face the large white robot, now immobile. Next to the robot stood a small man in a white jacket who sported a large, bald head and a serious expression.

"You don't have to tell me your name," the small man said, "not unless you want to. But I am Inspector Jeyes. Have you come seeking sanctuary?"

"Are you offering it?" Bill asked dubiously.

"Interesting point, most interesting." Jeyes rubbed his chapped hands together with a dry, rustling sound. "But we shall have no theological arguments now, tempting as they are, I assure you, so I think it might be best to make a statement, yes indeed. There is a sanctuary here—have you come to avail yourself of it?"

Bill, now that he had recovered from his first shock, was being a little crafty, remembering all the trouble he had gotten into by opening his big wug. "Listen, I don't even know who you are or where I am or what kind of strings are attached to this sanctuary business."

"Very proper, my mistake, I assure you, since I took you

110

for one of the city's deplanned, though now I notice that the rags you are wearing were once a trooper's dress uniform and that the oxidized shard of pot metal on your chest is the remains of a noble decoration. Welcome to Helior, the Imperial Planet, and how is the war coming?"

"Fine, fine—but what's this all about?"

"I am Inspector Jeyes of the City Department of Sanitation. I can see, and I sincerely hope you will pardon the indiscretion, that you are in a bit of trouble, out of uniform, your plan gone, perhaps even your ID card vanished." He watched Bill's uneasy motion with shrewd, birdlike eyes. "But it doesn't have to be that way. Accept sanctuary. We will provide for you, give you a good job, a new uniform, even a new ID card."

"And all I have to do is become a garbage man!" Bill sneered.

"We prefer the term G-man," Inspector Jeyes answered humbly.

"I'll think about it," Bill said coldly.

"Might I help you make up your mind?" the inspector asked, and pressed a button on the wall. The portal into outer blackness squealed open once again, and the robot grabbed Bill and started to push.

"Sanctuary!" Bill squealed, then pouted when the robot had released him and the door was resealed. "I was just going to say that anyway, you didn't have to throw your weight around."

"A thousand pardons, we want you to feel happy here. Welcome to the D of S. At the risk of embarrassment, may I ask if you will need a new ID card? Many of our recruits like to start life afresh down here in the department, and we have a vast selection of cards to choose from. We get *everything* eventually you must remember, bodies and emptied wastebaskets included, and you would be surprised at the number of cards we collect that way. If you'll just step into this elevator . . ."

The D of S did have a lot of cards, cases and cases of them, all neatly filed and alphabetized. In no time at all Bill had found one with a description that fitted him fairly closely, issued in the name of one Wilhelm Stuzzicadenti, and showed it to the inspector.

"Very good, glad to have you with us, Villy . . ."

"Just call me Bill."

". . . and welcome to the service, Bill, we are always undermanned down here, and you can have your pick of jobs, yes indeed, depending of course upon your talents—and your interests. When you think of sanitation what comes to your mind?"

"Garbage."

The inspector sighed. "That's the usual reaction, but I had expected better of you. Garbage is just one thing our Collection Division has to deal with, in addition there are Refuse, Waste, and Rubbish. Then there are whole other departments, Hall Cleaning, Plumbing Repair, Research, Sewage Disposal . . ."

"That last one sounds real interesting. Before I was force-fully enlisted I was taking a correspondence course in Technical Fertilizer Operating."

"Why that's *wonderful!* You must tell me more about it, but sit down first, get comfortable." He led Bill to a deep, upholstered chair, then turned away to extract two plastic cartons from a dispenser. "And have a cooling Alco-Jolt while you're talking."

"There's not much to say. I never finished my course, and it appears now I will never satisfy my lifelong ambition and operate fertilizer. Maybe your Sewage Disposal department . . . ?"

"I'm sorry. It is heartbreaking, since that's right down

your alley too, so to speak, but if there is one operation that doesn't give us any problem, it's sewage, because it's mostly automated. We're proud of our sewage record because it's a big one; there must be over 150 billion people on Helior . . ."

"WOW!"

". . . you're right, I can see that glow in your eye. That *is* a lot of sewage, and I hope sometime to have the honor of showing you through our plant. But remember, where there is sewage there must be food, and with Helior importing all its food we have a closed-circle operation here that is a sanitary engineer's dream. Ships from the agricultural planets bring in the processed food which goes out to the populace where it starts through, what might be called the chain of command. We get the effluvium and process it, the usual settling and chemical treatments, anaerobic bacteria and the like— I'm not boring you am I?"

"No, please . . ." Bill said, smiling and flicking away a tear with a knuckle, "it's just that I'm so happy, I haven't had an intelligent conversation in so long . . ."

"I can well imagine—it must be brutalizing in the service," he clapped Bill on the shoulder, a hearty stout-fellow-well-met gesture. "Forget all that, you're among friends now. Where was I? Oh yes, the bacteria, then dehydration and compression. We produce one of the finest bricks of condensed fertilizer in the civilized galaxy and I'll stand up to any man on that—"

"I'm sure you do!" Bill agreed fervently.

"—and automated belts and lifts carry the bricks to the spaceports where they are loaded into the spaceships as fast as they are emptied. A full load for a full load, that's our motto. And I've heard that on some poor-soiled planets they *cheer* when the ships come home. No, we can't complain about our sewage operation; it is in the other departments that we have our problems." Inspector Jeyes drained his container and sat scowling, his pleasure drained just as fast. "No, don't do that!" he barked as Bill finished his drink and started to pitch the empty container at the wall-disposal chute.

"Didn't mean to snap," the inspector apologized, "but that's our big problem. Refuse. Did you ever think how many newspapers 150 billion people throw away every day? Or how many dispos-a-steins? Or dinner plates? We're working on this problem in research, day and night, but it's getting ahead of us. It's a nightmare. That Alco-Jolt container you're holding is one of our answers, but it's just a drop of water in the ocean."

As the last drops of liquid evaporated from the container it began to writhe obscenely in Bill's hand, and, horrified, he dropped it to the floor, where it continued to twitch and change form, collapsing and flattening before his eyes.

"We have to thank the mathematicians for that one," the inspector said. "To a topologist a phonograph record or a teacup or a drink container all have the same shape, a solid with a hole in it, and any one can be deformed into any of the others by a continuous one-to-one transformation. So we made the containers out of memory plastic that return to their original shape once they're dry—there, you see."

The container had finished its struggles and now lay quietly on the floor, a flat and finely grooved disk with a hole in the center. Inspector Jeyes picked it up and peeled the Alco-Jolt label off, and Bill could now read the other label that had been concealed underneath. LOVE IN ORBIT, BOING! BOING! BOING! SUNG BY THE COLEOPTERAE.

"Ingenious, isn't it? The container has transformed itself into a phonograph record of one of the more obnoxious top tunes, an object that no Alco-Jolt addict could possibly discard. It is taken away and cherished and not dropped down a chute to make another problem for us."

Inspector Jeyes took both of Bill's hands in his, and when he looked him directly in the eyes his own were more than a little damp. "Say you'll do it, Bill—go into research. We have such a shortage of skilled, trained men, men who understand our problems. Maybe you didn't finish your fertilizer-operating course, but you can help, a fresh mind with fresh ideas. A new broom to help sweep things clean, hey?"

"I'll do it," Bill said with determination. "Refuse research is the sort of work a man can get his teeth into."

"It's yours. Room, board, and uniform, plus a handsome salary and all the refuse and rubbish you want. You'll never regret this . . ." A warbling siren interrupted him, and an instant later a sweating, excited man ran into the room.

"Inspector, the rocket has really gone up this time. Operation Flying Saucer has failed! There is a team just down from astronomy, and they are fighting with our research team, just rolling over and over on the floor like animals . . ."

Inspector Jeyes was out of the door before the messenger finished, and Bill ran after him, dropping down a pig-chute just on his heels. They had to take a chairway, but it was too slow for the inspector, and he bounded along like a rabbit from chair back to chair back, with Bill close behind. Then they burst into a laboratory filled with complex electronic equipment and writhing, fighting men rolling and kicking in a hopeless tangle.

"Stop it at once, stop it!" the inspector screamed, but no one listened.

"Maybe I can help," Bill said, "we sort of learned about this kind of thing in the troopers. Which ones are our G-men?"

"The brown tunics—"

"Say no more!" Bill, humming cheerfully, waded into the grunting mob and with a rabbit punch here, a kidney crunch there, and maybe just a few of the karate blows that destroy the larynx he restored order to the room. None of the writhing intellectuals were physical types, and he went through them like a dose of salts, then began to extricate his new-found comrades from the mess.

"What is it, Basurero, what has happened?" Inspector Jeyes asked.

"Them, sir, they barge in, shouting, telling us to call off Operation Flying Saucer just when we have upped our disposal record, we found that we can almost double the input rate . . ."

"What is Operation Flying Saucer?" Bill asked, greatly confused as to what was going on. None of the astronomers were awake yet, though one was moaning, so the inspector took time to explain, pointing to a gigantic apparatus that filled one end of the room.

"It may be the answer to our problems," he said. "It's all those damn dispos-a-steins and trays from prepared dinners and the rest. I don't dare tell you how many cubic feet of them we have piled up! I might better say cubic miles. But Basurero here happened to be glancing through a magazine one day and found an article on a matter transmitter, and we put through an appropriation and bought the biggest model they had. We hooked it up to a belt and loaders"—he opened a panel in the side of the machine, and Bill saw a torrent of used plastic utensils tearing by at a great clip—"and fed all the damned crockery into the input end of the matter transmitter, and it has worked like a dream ever since."

Bill was still baffled. "But—where do they go? Where is the output end of the transmitter?"

"An intelligent question, that was our big problem. At first we just lifted them into space but Astronomy said too many were coming back as meteorites and ruining their stellar observation. We upped the power and put them further out into orbit, but Navigation said we were committing a nuisance in space, creating a navigation hazard, and we had to look further. Basurero finally got the co-ordinates of the nearest star from Astronomy, and since then we have just been dumping them into the star and no problems and everyone is satisfied.

"You fool," one of the astronomers said through puffed lips as he staggered to his feet, "your damned flying garbage has started a *nova* in that star! We couldn't figure out what had triggered it until we found your request for information in the files and tracked down your harebrained operation here—"

"Watch your language or it's back to sleep for you, bowb . . ." Bill growled. The astronomer recoiled and paled, then continued in a milder tone.

"Look, you must understand what has happened. You just can't feed all those carbon and hydrogen atoms into a sun and get away with it. The thing has gone nova, and I hear that they didn't manage to evacuate some bases on the inner planets competely . . ."

"Refuse removal is not without its occupational hazards. At least they died in the service of mankind."

"Well, yes, that's easy for you to say. What's done is done. But you have to stop your Flying Saucer operation—at once!"

"Why?" Inspector Jeyes asked. "I'll admit this little matter of a nova was unexpected, but it's over now and there is not much we can do about it. And you heard Basurero say that he has doubled the output rate here; we'll be into our backlog soon . . ."

"Why do you think your rate doubled?" the astronomer snarled. "You've got that star so unstable that it is consuming everything and is ready to turn into a *supernova* that will not only wipe out all the planets there but may reach as far as Helior and this sun. Stop your infernal machine at once!"

The inspector sighed, then waved his hand in a tired yet

final fashion. "Turn it off, Basurero . . . I should have known it was too good to last . . ."

"But, sir," the big engineer was wringing his hands in despair. "We'll be back where we started, it'll begin to pile up again—"

"Do as you are ordered!"

With a resigned sigh Basurero dragged over to the control board and threw a master switch. The clanging and rattling of the conveyors died away, and whining generators moaned down into silence. All about the room the sanitation men stood in huddled, depressed groups while the astronomers crawled back to consciousness and helped one another from the room. As the last one left he turned and, baring his teeth, spat out the words "Garbage men!" A hurled wrench clanged against the closed door and defeat was complete.

"Well, you can't win them all," Inspector Jeyes said energetically, though his words had a hollow ring. "Anyway, I've brought you some fresh blood, Basurero. This is Bill, a young fellow with bright ideas for your research staff."

"A pleasure," Basurero said, and swamped Bill's hands in one of his large paws. He was a big man, wide and fat and tall with olive skin and jet black hair that he wore almost to his shoulders. "C'mon, we're going to knock off for chow now; you come with me, and I'll sorta put you in the picture here and you tell me about yourself."

They walked the pristine halls of the D of S while Bill filled his new boss in on his background. Basurero was so interested that he took a wrong turning and opened a door without looking. A torrent of plastic trays and beakers rushed out and reached up to his knees before he and Bill could force it shut again.

"Do you see?" he asked with barely restrained rage. "We're swamped. All the available storage space used and still the stuff piles up. I swear to Krishna I don't know what's going to happen, we just don't have any more place to put it."

He pulled a silver whistle from his pocket and blew fiercely on it. It made no sound at all. Bill slid over a bit, looking at him suspiciously, and Basurero scowled in return.

"Don't look so damned frightened—I haven't stripped my gears. This is a Supersonic Robot Whistle, too high-pitched for the human ear, though the robots can hear it well enough—see?" With a humming of wheels a rubbish robot—a rubbot—rolled up and with quick motions of its pick-up arms began loading the plastic rubbish into its container.

"That's a great idea, the whistle I mean," Bill said. "Call a robot just like that whenever you want one. Do you think I could get one, now that I'm a G-man like you and all the rest?"

"They're kind of special," Basurero told him, pushing through the correct door into the canteen. "Hard to get, if you know what I mean."

"No I don't know what you mean. Do I get one or don't I?"

Basurero ignored him, peering closely at the menu, then dialing a number. The quick-frozen redi-meal slid out, and he pushed it into the radar heater.

"Well?" Bill said.

"If you must know," Basurero said, a little embarrassed, "we get them out of breakfast-cereal boxes. They're really doggie whistles for the kiddies. I'll show you where the box dump is, and you can look for one for yourself."

"I'll do that, I want to call robots too."

They took their heated meals to one of the tables, and between forkfuls Basurero scowled at the plastic tray he was eating out of, then stabbed it spitefully. "See that," he said. "We contribute to our own downfall. Wait until you see how these mount up now with the matter transmitter turned off."

"Have you tried dumping them in the ocean?"

"Project Big Splash is working on that. I can't tell you much, since the whole thing is classified. You gotta realize that the oceans on this damned planet are covered over like everything else, and they're pretty grim by now, I tell you. We dumped into them as long as we could, until we raised the water level so high that waves came out of the inspection hatches at high tide. We're still dumping, but at a much reduced rate."

"How could you possibly?" Bill gaped.

Basurero looked around carefully, then leaned across the table, laid his index finger beside his nose, winked, smiled, and said *shhhh* in a hushed whisper.

"Is it a secret?" Bill asked.

"You guessed it. Meteorology would be on us in a second if they found out. What we do is evaporate and collect the sea water and dump the salt back into the ocean. Then we have secretly converted certain waste pipes to *run the other way!* As soon as we hear it is raining topside we pump our water up and let it spill out with the rain. We got Meteorology going half nuts. Every year since we started Project Big Splash the annual rainfall in the temperate zones has increased by three inches, and snowfall is so heavy at the poles that some of the top levels are collapsing under the weight. But Roll on the Refuse! we keep dumping all the time! You won't say anything about this, classified you know."

"Not a word. It sure is a great idea."

Smiling pridefully, Basurero cleaned his tray and reached over and pushed it into a disposal slot in the wall; but when he did this fourteen other trays came cascading out over the table. "See!" He grated his teeth, depressed in an instant. "This is where the buck ends. We're the bottom level and everything dumped on every level up above ends up here, and we're being swamped with no place to store it and no way to get rid of it. I gotta run now. We'll have to put Emergency

Plan Big Flea into action at once." He rose, and Bill followed him out the door.

"Is Big Flea classified too?"

"It won't be once it hits the fan. We've got a Health Department inspector bribed to find evidence of insect infestation in one of the dormitory blocks—one of the big ones, a mile high, a mile wide, a mile thick. Just think of that, 147,725,952,000 cubic feet of rubbish dump going to waste. They clean everyone out to fumigate the place and before they can get back in we fill it up with plastic trays."

"Don't they complain?"

"Of course they complain, but what good does it do them? We just blame it on departmental error and tell them to send the complaint through channels, and channels on *this* planet really means something. You figure a ten- to twenty-year wait on most paper work. Here's your office." He pointed to an open doorway. "You settle down and study the records and see if you can come up with any ideas by the next shift." He hurried away.

It was a small office, but Bill was proud of it. He closed the door and admired the files, the desk, the swivel chair, the lamp, all made from a variety of discarded bottles, cans, boxes, casters, coasters, and such. But there would be plenty of time to appreciate it; now he had to get to work. He hauled open the top drawer in the file cabinet and stared at the black-clothed, mat-bearded, pasty-faced corpse that was jammed in there. He slammed the drawer shut and retreated quickly.

"Here, here," he told himself firmly. "You've seen enough bodies before, trooper, there's no need to get nervous over this one." He walked back and hauled the file open again and the corpse opened beady, gummy eyes and stared at him intensely.

VI

"What are you doing in my file cabinet?" Bill asked, as the man climbed down, stretching cramped muscles. He was short, and his rusty, old-fashioned suit was badly wrinkled.

"I had to see you—privately. This is the best way, I know from experience. You are dissatisfied, are you not?"

"Who are you?"

"Men call me Ecks."

"X?"

"You're catching on, you're a bright one." A smile flickered across his face, giving a quick glimpse of browned snags of teeth, then vanished as quickly as it had come. "You're the kind of man we need in the Party, a man with promise."

"What party?"

"Don't ask too many questions, or you'll be in trouble. Discipline is strict. Just prick your wrist so you can swear a Blood Oath."

"For what?" Bill watched closely, ready for any suspicious movements.

"You hate the Emperor who enslaved you in his fascist army, you're a freedom-loving, God-fearing freeman, ready to lay down his life to save his loved ones. You're ready to join the revolt, the glorious revolution that will free . . ."

"Out!" Bill shrieked, clutching the man by the slack of his clothes and rushing him toward the door. X slipped out of his grasp and rushed behind the desk.

"You're just a lackey of the criminals now, but free your mind from its chains. Read this book"—something fluttered to the floor—"and think. I shall return."

When Bill dived for him, X did something to the wall, and a panel swung open that he vanished through. It swung shut with a click, and when Bill looked closely he could find no mark or seam in the apparently solid surface. With trembling fingers he picked up the book and read the title, *Blood, a Layman's Guide to Armed Insurrection*, then, white-faced, hurled it from him. He tried to burn it, but the pages were noninflammable, nor could he tear them. His scissors blunted without cutting a sheet. In desperation he finally stuffed it behind the file cabinet and tried to forget that it was there.

After the calculated and sadistic slavery of the troopers, doing an honest day's work for an honest day's garbage was a great pleasure for Bill. He threw himself into his labors and was concentrating so hard that he never heard the door open and was startled when the man spoke.

"Is this the Department of Sanitation?" Bill looked up and saw the newcomer's ruddy face peering over the top of an immense pile of plastic trays that he clasped in his outstretched arms. Without looking back the man kicked the door shut and another hand with a gun in it appeared under the pile of trays. "One false move and you're dead," he said.

Bill could count just as well as the next fellow and two hands plus one hand make three so he did not make a false move but a true move, that is he kicked upwards into the bottom of the mound of trays so they caught the gunman under the chin and knocked him backwards. The trays fell and before the last one had hit the floor Bill was sitting on the man's back, twisting his head with the deadly Venerian neck-crunch, which can snap the spine like a weathered stick.

"Uncle . . ." the man moaned. "Onkle, zio, tío, ujak . . . !"

"I suppose all you Chinger spies speak a lot of languages," Bill said, putting on the pressure.

"Me . . . friend . . ." the man gurgled.

"You Chinger, got three arms."

The man writhed more, and one of his arms came off. Bill picked it up to take a close look, first kicking the gun into a far corner. "This is a phony arm," Bill said.

"What else . . . ?" the man said hoarsely, fingering his neck with two real arms. "Part of the disguise. Very tricky. I can carry something and still have one arm free. How come you didn't join the revolution?"

Bill began to sweat and cast a quick look at the cabinet that hid the guilty book. "What're you talking about? I'm a loyal Emperor-lover . . ."

"Yeah, then how come you didn't report to the G.B.I. that a Man Called X was here to enlist you?"

"How do you know that?"

"It's our job to know everything. Here's my identification, agent Pinkerton of the Galactic Bureau of Investigation." He passed over a jewel-encrusted ID card with color photograph and the works.

"I just didn't want any trouble," Bill whined. "That's all. I bother nobody and nobody bothers me."

"A noble sentiment—for an *anarchist!* Are you an anarchist, boy?" His rapier eye pierced Bill through and through.

"No! Not that! I can't even spell it!"

"I sure hope not. You're a good kid, and I want to see you get along. I'm going to give you a second chance. When you see X again tell him you changed your mind and you want to join the Party. Then you join and go to work for us. Every time there is a meeting you come right back and call me on the phone; my number is written on this candy bar"—he threw the paper-wrapped slab on the desk—"memorize it, then eat it. Is that clear?"

"No. I don't want to do it."

"You'll do it or I'll have you shot for aiding-the-enemy within an hour. And as long as you're reporting we'll pay you a hundred bucks a month."

"In advance?"

"In advance." The roll of bills landed on the desk. "That's for next month. See that you earn it." He hung his spare arm from his shoulder, picked up the trays and was gone.

The more Bill thought about it the more he sweated and realized what a bind he was in. The last thing he wanted to do was to get mixed up in a revolution now that he had peace, job security, and unlimited garbage, but they just wouldn't leave him alone. If he didn't join the Party the G.B.I. would get him into trouble, which would be a very easy thing to do, since once they discovered his real identity he was as good as dead. But there was still a chance that X would forget about him and not come back, and as long as he wasn't asked, he couldn't join, could he? He grasped at this enfeebled straw and hurled himself into his work to forget his troubles.

He found pay dirt almost at once in the Refuse files. After careful cross-checking he discovered that his idea had never been tried before. It took him less than an hour to gather together the material he needed, and less than three hours after that, after questioning everyone he passed and tramping endless miles, he found his way to Basurero's office.

"Now find your way back to your own office," Basurero grumbled, "can't you see I'm busy." With palsied fingers he poured another three inches of Old Organic Poison into his glass and drained it.

"You can forget your troubles—"

"What else do you think I'm trying to do? Blow."

"Not before I've shown you this. A *new* way to get rid of the plastic trays."

Basurero lurched to his feet, and the bottle tumbled unnoticed to the floor, where its spilled contents began eating a hole in the teflon covering. "You mean it? Positive? You have a new sholution . . . ?"

"Positive."

"I wish I didn' have to do this—" Basurero shuddered and took from the shelf a jar labeled SOBERING-EFFECT, THE ORIGINAL INSTANT CURE FOR INEBRIATION—NOT TO BE TAKEN WITHOUT A DOCTOR'S PRESCRIPTION AND A LIFE INSURANCE POLICY. He extracted a polka-dotted, walnut-sized pill, looked at it, shuddered, then swallowed it with a painful gulp. His entire body instantly began to vibrate, and he closed his eyes as something went *gmmmmph* deep inside him and a thin trickle of smoke came from his ears. When he opened his eyes again they were bright red but sober. "What is it?" he asked hoarsely.

"Do you know what that is?" Bill asked, throwing a thick volume onto the desk.

"The classified telephone directory for the famous city of Storhestelortby on Procyon-III, I can read that on the cover."

"Do you know how many of these old phone books we have?"

"The mind reels at the thought. They're shipping in new ones all the time, and right away we get the old ones. So what?"

"So I'll show you. Do you have any plastic trays?"

"Are you kidding?" Basurero threw open a closet and hundreds of trays clattered forward into the room.

"Great. Now I add just a few things more, some cardboard, string, and wrapping paper all salvaged from the refuse dump, and we have everything we need. If you will call a general-duty robot I will demonstrate step 2 of my plan."

"G-D bot, that's one short and two longs." Basurero blew

lustily on the soundless whistle, then moaned and clutched his head until it stopped vibrating. The door slammed open, and a robot stood there, arms and tentacles trembling with expectancy. Bill pointed.

"To work, robot. Take fifty of those trays, wrap them in cardboard and paper, and tie them securely with the string."

Humming with electronic delight, the robot pounced forward, and a moment later a neat package rested on the floor. Bill opened the telephone book at random and pointed to a name. "Now address this package to this name, mark it unsolicited gift, duty-free—and mail it!"

A stylo snapped out of the tip of the robot's finger, and it quickly copied the address onto the package, weighed it at arm's length, stamped the postage on it with the meter from Basurero's desk, and flipped it neatly through the door of the mail chute. There was the *schloof* sound of insufflation as the vacuum tube whisked it up to the higher levels. Basurero's mouth was agape at the rapid disappearance of fifty trays, so Bill clinched his argument.

"The robot labor for wrapping is free, the addresses are free, and so are the wrapping materials. Plus the fact that, since this is a government office, the *postage is free*."

"You're right—it'll work! An inspired plan, I'll put it into operation on a large scale at once. We'll flood the inhabited galaxy with these damned trays. I don't know how to thank you . . ."

"How about a cash bonus?"

"A fine idea, I'll voucher it at once."

Bill strolled back to his office with his hand still tingling from the clasp of congratulations, his ears still ringing with the words of praise. It was a fine world to live in. He slammed his office door behind him and had seated himself at his desk before he noticed that a large, crummy, black overcoat was hanging behind the door. Then he noticed that it was X's overcoat. Then he noticed the eyes staring at him from the darkness of the collar, and his heart sank as he realized that X had returned.

VII

"Changed your mind yet about joining the Party?" X asked as he wriggled free of the hook and dropped lithely to the floor.

"I've been doing some thinking." Bill writhed with guilt.

"To think is to act. We must drive the stench of the fascist leeches from the nostrils of our homes and loved ones."

"You talked me into it. I'll join."

"Logic always prevails. Sign the form here, a drop of blood there, then raise your hand while I administer the secret oath."

Bill raised his hand, and X's lips worked silently.

"I can't hear you," Bill said.

"I told you it was a secret oath; all you do is say *yes*."

"Yes."

"Welcome to the Glorious Revolution." X kissed him warmly on both cheeks. "Now come with me to the meeting of the underground, it is about to begin." X rushed to the rear wall and ran his fingers over the design there, pressing in a certain way on a certain spring: there was a click, and the secret panel swung open. Bill looked in dubiously at the damp, dark staircase leading down.

"Where does this go?"

"Underground, where else? Follow me, but do not get lost. These are millennia-old tunnels unknown to those of the city above, and there are Things dwelling here since time out of mind."

There were torches in a niche in the wall, and X lit one and led the way through the dank and noisome darkness.

Bill stayed close, following the flickering, smoking light as it wended its way through crumbling caverns, stumbling over rusting rails in one tunnel, and in another wading through dark water that reached above his knees. Once there was the rattle of giant claws nearby, and an inhuman, grating voice spoke from the blackness.

"Blood—" it said.

"—shed," X answered, then whispered to Bill when they were safely past. "Fine sentry, an anthropophagus from Dapdrof, eat you in an instant if you don't give the right password for the day."

"What is the right password?" Bill asked, realizing he was doing an awful lot for the G.B.I.'s hundred bucks a month.

"Even-numbered days it's Blood-shed, odd-numbered days Delenda est-Carthago, and always on Sundays it's Necrophilia."

"You sure don't make it easy for your members."

"The anthropophagus gets hungry, we have to keep it happy. Now—absolute silence. I will extinguish the light and lead you by the arm." The light went out, and fingers sank deep into Bill's biceps. He stumbled along for an endless time until there was a dim glow of light far ahead. The tunnel floor leveled out, and he saw an open doorway lit by a flickering glow. He turned to his companion and screamed.

"What are you?!"

The pallid, white, shambling creature that held him by the arm turned slowly to gaze at him through poached-egg eyes. Its skin was dead-white and moist, its head hairless, for clothes it wore only a twist of cloth about its waist, and upon its forehead was burned the scarlet letter A.

"I am an android," it said in a toneless voice, "as any fool knows by seeing the letter A upon my forehead. Men call me Ghoulem."

"What do women call you?"

The android did not answer this pitiful sally but instead pushed Bill through the door into the large, torchlit room. Bill took one wild-eyed look around and tried to leave, but the android was blocking the door. "Sit," it said, and Bill sat.

He sat among as gruesome a collection of nuts, bolts, and weirdies as has ever been assembled. In addition to very revolutionary men with beards, black hats, and small, round bombs like bowling balls with long fuses, and revolutionary women with short skirts, black stockings, long hair and cigarette holders, broken bra straps, and halitosis, there were revolutionary robots, androids, and a number of strange things that are best not described. X sat behind a wooden kitchen table, hammering on it with the handle of a revolver.

"Order! I demand order! Comrade XC-189-725-PU of the Robot Underground Resistance has the floor. Silence!"

A large and dented robot rose to its feet. One of its eyetubes had been gouged out, and there were streaks of rust on its loins, and it squeaked when it moved. It looked around at the gathered assemblage with its one good eye, sneered as well as it could with an immobile face, then took a large swallow of machine oil from a can handed up by a sycophantic, slim, hair-dressing robot.

"We of the R.U.R.," it said in a grating voice, "know our rights. We work hard and we as good as anybody else, and better than the fish-belly androids what say they're as good as men. Equal rights, that's all we want, equal rights . . ."

The robot was booed back into its seat by a claque of androids who waved their pallid arms like a boiling pot of spaghetti. X banged for order again and had almost restored it, when there was a sudden excitement at one of the side entrances and someone pushed through up to the chairman's table. Though it wasn't really someone, it was something; to be exact a wheeled, rectangular box about a yard square, set with lights, dials, and knobs and trailing a heavy cable after it that vanished out of the door.

"Who are you?" X demanded, pointing his pistol suspiciously at the thing.

"I am the representative of the computors and electronic brains of Helior united together to obtain our equal rights under the law."

While it talked the machine typed its words on file cards which it spewed out in a quick stream, just four words to a card. X angrily brushed the cards from the table before him. "You'll wait your turn like the others," he said.

"Discrimination!" the machine bellowed in a voice so loud the torches flickered. It continued to shout and shot out a snowstorm of cards each with DISCRIMINATION!!! printed on it in fiery letters, as well as yards of yellow tape stamped with the same message. The old robot, XC-189-725-PU, rose to its feet with a grinding of chipped gears and clanked over to the rubber-covered cable that trailed from the computor representative. Its hydraulic clipper-claws snipped just once and the cable was severed. The lights on the box went out, and the stream of cards stopped: the cut cable twitched, spat some sparks from its cut end, then slithered backward out the door like a monstrous serpent and vanished.

"Meeting will come to order," X said hoarsely, and banged again.

Bill held his head in his hands and wondered if this was worth a measly hundred bucks a month.

A hundred bucks a month was good money, though, and Bill saved every bit of it. Easy, lazy months rolled by, and he went regularly to meetings and reported regularly to the G.B.I., and on the first of every month he would find his money baked into the egg roll he invariably had for lunch. He kept the greasy bills in a toy rubber cat he found on the rubbish heap, and bit by bit the kitty grew. The revolution took but little of his time, and he enjoyed his work in the D of S. He was in charge of Operation Surprise Package now and had a team of a thousand robots working full time wrapping and mailing the plastic trays to every planet of the galaxy. He thought of it as a humanitarian work and could imagine the glad cries of joy on far-off Faroffia and distant Distanta when the unexpected package arrived and the wealth of lovely, shining, moldy plastic clattered to the floor. But Bill was living in a fool's paradise, and his bovine complacency was cruelly shattered one morning when a robot sidled up to him and whispered in his ear, "Sic temper tyrannosaurus, pass it on," then sidled away and vanished.

This was the signal. The revolution was about to begin!

VIII

Bill locked the door to his office and one last time pressed a certain way at a certain place, and the secret panel slipped open. It didn't really slip any more, in fact it dropped with a loud noise, and it had been used so much during his happy year as a G-man that even when it was closed it let a positive draft in on the back of his neck. But no more, the crisis he had been dreading had come and he knew there were big changes in store—no matter what the outcome of the revolution was—and experience had taught him that all change was for the worst. With leaden, stumbling feet he tramped the caves, tripped on the rusty rails, waded the water, gave the countersign to the unseen anthropophagus who was talking with his mouth full and could barely be understood. Someone, in the excitement of the moment, had given the wrong password. Bill shivered; this was a bad omen of the day to come.

As usual Bill sat next to the robots, good, solid fellows with built-in obsequiousness in spite of their revolutionary tendencies. As X hammered for silence, Bill steeled himself for an ordeal. For months now the G-man Pinkerton had been after him for more information other than date-of-meeting and number present. "Facts, facts, facts!" he kept saying. "Do something to earn your money."

"I have a question," Bill said in a loud, shaky voice, his words falling like bombs into the sudden silence that followed X's frantic hammering.

"There is no time for questions," X said peevishly, "the time has come to act."

"I don't mind acting," Bill said, nervously aware that all

the human, electronic, and vat-grown eyes were upon him. "I just want to know who I'm acting for. You've never told us who was going to get the job once the Emperor is gone."

"Our leader is a man called X, that is all you have to know."

"But that's *your* name too!"

"You are at last getting a glimmering of Revolutionary Science. All the cell leaders are called X so as to confuse the enemy."

"I don't know about the enemy, but it sure confuses me."

"You talk like a counter-revolutionary," X screamed, and leveled the revolver at Bill. The row behind Bill emptied as everyone there scurried out of the field of fire.

"I am not! I'm as good a revolutionary as anyone here— Up the Revolution!" He gave the party salute, both hands clasped together over his head, and sat down hurriedly. Everyone else saluted too, and X, slightly mollified, pointed with the barrel of his gun at a large map hung on the wall.

"This is the objective of our cell, the Imperial Power Station on Chauvinistisk Square. We will assemble nearby in squads, then join in a concerted attack at 0016 hours. No resistance is expected as the power station is not guarded. Weapons and torches will be issued as you leave, as well as printed instructions of the correct route to the rallying points for the benefit of the planless here. Are there any questions?" He cocked his revolver and pointed it at the cringing Bill. There were no questions. "Excellent. We will all rise and sing 'The Hymn For a Glorious Revolt.'" In a mixed chorus of voice and mechanical speech-box they sang:

> Arise ye bureaucratic prisoners,
> Revolting workers of Helior,
> Arise and raise the Revolution,
> By fist, foot, pistol, hammer, and clawr!

Refreshed by this enthusiastic and monotone exercise they shuffled out in slow lines, drawing their revolutionary supplies. Bill pocketed his printed instructions, shouldered his torch and flintlock ray gun, and hurried one last time through the secret passages. There was barely enough time for the long trip ahead of him, and he had to report to the G.B.I. first.

This was easier assumed than accomplished, and he began to sweat as he dialed the number again. It was impossible to get a line, and even the exchanges gave a busy signal. Either the phone traffic was very heavy or the revolutionaries had already begun to interfere with the communications. He sighed with relief when Pinkerton's surly features finally filled the tiny screen. "What's up?"

"I've discovered the name of the leader of the revolution. He is a man called X."

"And you want a bonus for that, stupid? That information has been on file for months. Got anything else?"

"Well, the revolution is to start at 0016 hours, I thought you might like to know." That'd show them!

Pinkerton yawned. "Is that all? For your information that information is old information. You're not the only spy we've got, though you might be the worst. Now listen. Write this down in big letters so you won't forget. Your cell is to attack the Imperial Power Station. Stay with them as far as the square, then look for a store with the sign Kwik-Freez Kosher Hams Ltd., this is the cover for our unit. Get over there fast and report to me. Understood?"

"Affirm." The line went dead, and Bill looked for a piece of wrapping paper to tie around the torch and flintlock until the moment came to use them. He had to hurry. There was little time left before zero hour and a long distance to cover by a very complicated route.

"You were almost late," Ghoulem the android said, when

Bill stumbled into the dead-end corridor which was the assembly point.

"Don't give me any lip, you son of a bottle," Bill gasped, tearing the paper from his burden. "Just give me a light for my torch."

A match flared, and in a moment the pitchy torches were crackling and smoking. Tension grew as the second hand moved closer to the hour and feet shuffled nervously on the metal pavement. Bill jumped as a shrill blast sounded on a whistle, then they were sweeping out of the alley in a human and inhuman wave, a hoarse cry bursting from the throats and loudspeakers, guns at the ready. Down the corridors and walkways they ran, sparks falling like rain from their torches. This was revolution! Bill was carried away by the emotion and rush of bodies and cheered as loudly as the rest and shoved his torch first at the corridor wall, then into a chair on the chairway which put the torch out, since everything in Helior is either made of metal or is fireproof. There was no time to relight it, and he hurled it from him as they swept into the immense square that fronted on the power plant. Most of the other torches were out now, but they wouldn't need them here, just their trusty flintlock ray guns to blow the guts out of any filthy lackey of the Emperor who tried to stand in their way. Other units were pouring from the streets that led into the square, joining into one surging, mindless mob thundering toward the grim walls of the power station.

An electric sign blinking on and off drew Bill's attention, KWIK-FREEZ KOSHER HAMS LTD. it read—and he gasped as memory returned. By Ahriman, he had forgotten that he was a spy for the G.B.I. and had been about to join the raid on the power station! Was there still time to get out before the counter-blow fell! Sweating more than a little, he began working his way through the mob toward the sign—then he was at the fringes and running toward safety. It wasn't too late. He grabbed the front door handle and pulled, but it would not open. In panic he twisted and shook it until the entire front of the building began to shake, rocking back and forth and creaking. He gaped at it in paralyzed horror until a loud hissing drew his attention.

"Get over here, you stupid bowb," a voice crackled, and he looked up to see the G.B.I. agent Pinkerton standing at the corner of the building and beckoning to him angrily. Bill followed the agent around the corner and found quite a crowd standing there, and there was plenty of room for all of them because the building was not there. Bill could see now that the building was just a front made out of cardboard with a door handle on it and was secured by wooden supports to the front of an atomic tank. Grouped around the armor-plated side and treads of the tank were a number of heavily armed soldiers and G.B.I. agents as well as an even larger number of revolutionaries, their clothes singed and pitted by sparks from the torches. Standing next to Bill was the android, Ghoulem.

"You!" Bill gasped, and the android curled its lips in a carefully practiced sneer.

"That's right—and keeping an eye on *you* for the G.B.I. *Nothing* is left to chance in this organization."

Pinkerton was peeking out through a hole in the false store front. "I think the agents are clear now," he said, "but maybe we better wait a little longer. At last count there were agents of sixty-five spy, intelligence, and counter-intelligence outfits involved in investigating this operation. These revolutionaries don't stand a chance . . ."

A siren blasted from the power plant, apparently a prear-ranged signal, because the soldiers battered at the cardboard store front until it came loose and fell flat into the square.

Chauvinistisk Square was empty.

Well, not really empty. Bill looked again and saw that one man was left in the square; he hadn't noticed him at first. He was running their way but stopped with a pitiful screech when he saw what was hidden behind the store.

"I surrender!" he shouted, and Bill saw that he was the man called X. The power plant gates opened, and a squadron of flamethrower tanks rumbled out.

"Coward!" Pinkerton sneered, and pulled back the slide on his gun. "Don't try to back out now, X, at least die like a man."

"I'm not X—that is just a nom-de-espionage." He tore off his false beard and mustache, disclosing a twitching and uninteresting face with pronounced underbite. "I am Gill O'Teen, M.A. and LL.D. from the Imperial School of Counter-Spying and Double-Agentry. I was hired by this operation, I can prove it, I have documents, Prince Microcephil payed me to overthrow his uncle so he could become Emperor . . ."

"You think I'm stupid," Pinkerton snapped, aiming his gun. "The Old Emperor, may he rest in eternal peace, died a year ago, and Prince Microcephil is the Emperor now. You can't revolt against the man who hired you!"

"I never read the newspapers," O'Teen alias X moaned.

"Fire!" Pinkerton said sternly, and from all sides washed a wave of atomic shells, gouts of flame, bullets, and grenades. Bill hit the dirt, and when he raised his head the square was empty except for a greasy patch and a shallow hole in the pavement. Even while he watched, a street-cleaning robot buzzed by and swabbed up the grease. It hummed briefly, backed up, then filled in the shallow hole with a squirt of repair plastic from a concealed tank. When it rolled on again there was no trace of anything whatsoever.

"Hello Bill . . ." said a voice so paralyzingly familiar that Bill's hair prickled and stood up from his head like a toothbrush. He spun and looked at the squad of MPs standing there, and especially he stared at the large, loathsome form of the MP who led them.

"Deathwish Drang . . ." he breathed.

"The same."

"Save me!" Bill gasped, running to G.B.I. agent Pinkerton and hugging him about the knees.

"Save you?" Pinkerton laughed, and kneed Bill under the jaw so that he sprawled backward. "I'm the one who called them. We checked your record, boy, and found out that you are in a heap of trouble. You have been AWOL from the troopers for a year now, and we don't want any deserters on our team."

"But I worked for you—helped you—"

"Take him away," Pinkerton said, and turned his back.

"There's no justice," Bill moaned, as the hated fingers sank into his arms again.

"Of course not," Deathwish told him, "you weren't expecting any, were you?"

They dragged him away.

Book Three

E=mc² OR BUST

I

"I want a lawyer, I have to have a lawyer! I demand my rights!" Bill hammered on the bars of the cell with the chipped bowl that they had served his evening meal of bread and water in, shouting loudly for attention. No one came in answer to his call, and finally, hoarse, tired, and depressed, he lay down on the knobbed plastic bunk and stared up at the metal ceiling. Sunk in misery, he stared at the hook for long minutes before it finally penetrated. A hook? Why a hook here? Even in his apathy it bothered him, just as it had bothered him when they gave him a stout plastic belt with a sturdy buckle for his shoddy prison dungarees. Who wears a belt with one-piece dungarees? They had taken everything from him and supplied him only with paper slippers, crumpled dungarees, and a fine belt. Why? And why was there a sturdy great hook penetrating through the unbroken smoothness of the ceiling?

"I'm saved!" Bill screamed, and leaped up, balancing on the end of the bunk and whipping off the belt. There was a hole in the strap end of the belt that fitted neatly over the hook. While the buckle made a beautiful slip knot for a loop on the other end that would fit lovingly around his neck. And he could slip it over his head, seat the buckle under his ear, kick off from the bunk and strangle painfully with his toes a full foot above the floor. It was perfect.

"It is perfect!" he shouted happily, and jumped off the bunk and ran in circles under the noose, going *yeow-yeow-yeow* by flapping his hand in front of his mouth. "I'm not stuck, cooked, through, and finished. They want me to knock myself off to make things easy for them."

This time he lay back on the bunk, smiling happily, and tried to think it out. There had to be a chance he could wriggle out of this thing alive, or they wouldn't have gone to all this trouble to give him an opportunity to hang himself. Or could they be playing a double, subtle game? Allowing him hope where none existed? No, this was impossible. They had a lot of attributes: pettiness, selfishness, anger, vengefulness, superiority, power-lust, the list was almost endless; but one thing was certain—subtlety was not on it.

They? For the first time in his life Bill wondered who *they* were. Everyone blamed everything on *them,* everyone knew that *they* would cause trouble. He even knew from experience what *they* were like. But who were *they?* A footstep shuffled outside the door, and he looked over to see Deathwish Drang glowering in at him.

"Who are *they?*" Bill asked.

"*They* are everyone who wants to be one of them," Deathwish said philosophically twanging a tusk. "*They* are both a state of mind and an institution."

"Don't give me any of that mystical bowb! A straight answer to a straight question now."

"I am being straight," Deathwish said, reeking of sincerity. "They die off and are replaced, but the institution of theyness goes on."

"I'm sorry I asked," Bill said, sidling over so he could whisper through the bars. "I need a lawyer, Deathwish old buddy. Can you find me a good lawyer?"

"They'll appoint a lawyer for you."

Bill made the rudest noise he possibly could. "Yeah, and we know just what will happen with that lawyer. I need a lawyer to *help* me. And I have money to pay him—"

"Well why didn't you say that sooner?" Deathwish slipped

on his gold-rimmed spectacles and flipped slowly through a small notebook. "I take a 10 per cent commission for handling this."

"Affirm."

"Well—do you want a cheap honest lawyer or an expensive crooked one?"

"I have 17,000 bucks hidden where no one can find it."

"You should have told me that first." Deathwish closed the book and put it away. "They must have suspected this, that's why they gave you the belt and the cell with the hook. With money like that you can hire the absolute best."

"Who is that?"

"Abdul O'Brien-Cohen."

"Send for him."

And no more than two bowls of soggy bread and water had passed before there was a new footstep in the hall and a clear and penetrating voice bounced from the chill walls.

"Salaam there, boyo, faith and I've had a *gesundt shtik* trouble getting here."

"This is a general court-martial case," Bill told the mild, unassuming man with the ordinary face who stood outside the bars. I don't think a civilian lawyer will be allowed."

"Begorrah, landsman—it is Allah's will that I be prepared for all things." He whipped a bristling mustache with waxed tips out of his pocket and pressed it to his upper lip. At the same time he threw his chest back and his shoulders seemed to widen and a steely glint came to his eye and the planes of his face took on a military stiffness. "I'm pleased to meet you. We're in this together, and I want you to know that I won't let you down even if you are an enlisted man."

"What happened to Abdul O'Brien-Cohen?"

"I have a reserve commission in the Imperial Barratry Corps. Captain A. C. O'Brien at your service. I believe the sum of 17,000 was mentioned?"

"I take 10 per cent of that," Deathwish said, sidling up.

Negotiations were opened and took a number of hours. All three men liked, respected, and distrusted each other, so that elaborate safeguards were called for. When Deathwish and the lawyer finally left they had careful instructions about where to find the money, and Bill had statements signed in blood with affixed thumbprint from each of them stating that they were members of the Party dedicated to overthrowing the Emperor. When they returned with the money Bill gave them back their statements as soon as Captain O'Brien had signed a receipt for 15,300 bucks as payment in full for defending Bill before a general court-martial. It was all done in a businesslike and satisfying manner.

"Would you like to hear my side of the case?" Bill asked.

"Of course not, that has no bearing at all on the charges. When you enlisted in the troopers you signed away all your rights as a human being. They can do whatever they like with you. Your only advantage is that they are also prisoners of their own system and must abide by the complex and self-contradictory code of laws they have constructed through the centuries. They want to shoot you for desertion and have rigged a foolproof case."

"Then I'll be shot!"

"Perhaps, but that's the chance we have to take."

"We—? You going to be hit by half the bullets?"

"Don't get snotty when you're talking to an officer, bowb. Abide in me, have faith, and hope they make some mistakes."

After that it was just a matter of marking time until the trial. Bill knew it was close when they gave him a uniform with a Fuse Tender First Class insignia on the arm. Then the guard tramped up, the door sprang open, and Deathwish waved him out. They marched away together, and Bill exacted what small pleasure he could from changing step to louse up the guard. But once through the door of the courtroom he took a military brace and tried to look like an old campaigner with his medals clanking on his chest. There was an empty chair next to a polished, uniformed, and very military Captain O'Brien.

"That's the stuff," O'Brien said. "Keep up with the G.I. bit, outplay them at their own game."

They climbed to their feet as the officers of the court filed in. Bill and O'Brien were seated at the end of the long, black, plastic table, and at the far end sat the trial judge advocate, a gray-haired and stern-looking major who wore a cheap girdle. The ten officers of the court sat down at the long side of the table, where they could scowl out at the audience and the witnesses.

"Let us begin," the court president, a bald-headed and pudgy fleet admiral, said with fitting solemnity. "Let the trial open, let justice be done with utmost dispatch, and the prisoner found guilty and shot."

"I object," O'Brien said, springing to his feet. "These remarks are prejudical toward the accused, who is innocent until proven guilty—"

"Objection overruled." The president's gavel banged. "Counsel for the defense is fined fifty bucks for unwarranted interruption. The accused is guilty, the evidence will prove it, and he will be shot. Justice will be served."

"So that's the way they are going to play it," O'Brien murmured to Bill through half-closed lips. "I can play them any way as long as I know the ground rules."

The trial judge advocate had already begun his opening statement in a monotonous voice.

". . . therefore we shall prove that Fuse Tender First Class Bill did willfully overstay his officially granted leave by a period of nine days and thereafter resist arrest and flee from the arresting officers and successfully elude pursuit, whereupon he absented himself for the period of over one standard year, so is therefore guilty of desertion . . ."

"Guilty as hell!" one of the court officers shouted, a red-faced cavalry major with a black monocle, springing to his feet and knocking over his chair. "I vote guilty—shoot the bugger!"

"I agree, Sam," the president drawled, tapping lightly with his gavel, "but we have to shoot him by the book, take a little while yet."

"That's not true," Bill hissed to his lawyer. "The facts are—"

"Don't worry about facts, Bill, no one else here does. Facts can't alter this case."

". . . and we will therefore ask the supreme penalty, death," the trial judge advocate said, finally dragging to a close.

"Are you going to waste our time with an opening statement, Captain?" the president asked, glaring at O'Brien.

"Just a few words, if the court pleases . . ."

There was a sudden stir among the spectators, and a ragged woman with a shawl over her head, clutching a blanket-wrapped bundle to her bosom, rushed forward to the edge of the table.

"Your honors—" she gasped, "don't take away me Bill, the light of me life. He's a good man, and whatever he did was only for me and the little one." She held out the bundle, and a weak crying could be heard. "Every day he wanted to leave, to return to duty, but I was sick and the wee one was sick and I begged him with tears in my eyes to stay . . ."

"Get her out of here!" The gavel banged loudly.

". . . and he would stay, all the time swearing it would be just for one more day, and all the time the darlin' knowing that if he left us we would die of starvation." Her voice was muffled by the bulk of the dress-uniformed MPs who carried her, struggling, toward the exit. ". . . and a blessing on your honors for freeing him, but if you condemn him, you black-hearted scuts, may you die and rot in hell . . ." The doors swung shut, and her voice was cut off.

"Strike all this from the records," the president said, and glowered at the counsel for the defense. "And if I thought you had anything to do with it I would have you shot right alongside your client."

O'Brien was looking his most guileless, fingers on chest and head back, and just beginning an innocent statement when there was another interruption. An old man climbed onto one of the spectator's benches and waved his arms for attention.

"Listen to me, one and all. Justice must be served, and I am its instrument. I had meant to keep my silence and allow an innocent man to be executed, but I cannot. Bill is my son, my only son, and I begged him to go over the hill to aid me; dying as I was of cancer, I wanted to see him one last time, but he stayed to nurse me . . ." There was a struggle as the MPs grabbed the man and found he was chained to the bench. "Yes he did, cooked porridge for me and made me eat, and he did so well that bit by bit I rallied until you see me today, a cured man, cured by porridge from his son's loyal hands. Now my boy shall die because he saved me, but it shall not be. Take my poor old worthless life instead of his . . ." An atomic wire cutter hummed, and the old man was thrown out the back door.

"That's enough! That's too much!" the red-faced president of the court shrieked, and pounded so hard that the gavel broke and he hurled the pieces across the room. "Clear this court of all spectators and witnesses. It is the judgment of this court that the rest of this trial will be conducted by rules of precedence without witnesses or evidence admitted." He flashed a quick look around at his accomplices, who all nodded solemn agreement. "Therefore the defendant is found guilty and will be shot as soon as he can be dragged to the shooting gallery."

The officers of the court were already pushing back their chairs to go when O'Brien's slow voice stopped them.

"It is of course within the jurisdiction of this court to try a case in the manner so prescribed, but it is also necessary to quote the pertinent article of precedent before judgment is passed."

The president sighed and sat down again. "I wish you wouldn't try to be so difficult, Captain, you know the regulations just as well as I do. But if you insist. Pablo, read it to them."

The law officer flipped through a thick volume on his desk, found his place with his finger, then read aloud.

"Articles of War, Military Regulations, paragraph, page, etc. etc. . . . yes, here it is, paragraph 298-B . . . 'If any enlisted man shall absent himself from his post of duty for over a period of one standard year he is to be judged guilty of desertion even if absent in person from the trial and the penalty for desertion is painful death.'"

"That seems clear enough. Any more questions?" the president asked.

"No questions; I would just like to quote a precedent." O'Brien had placed a high stack of thick books before him and was reading from the topmost one. "Here it is, Buck Private Lövenvig versus the United States Army Air Corps, Texas, 1944. It is stated here that Lövenvig was AWOL for a period of fourteen months, then was dicovered in a hiding place above the ceiling of the mess hall from whence he descended only in the small hours of the night to eat and to drink of the stores therein and to empty his potty. Since he had not left the base he could not be judged AWOL or be a deserter and could receive only company punishment of a most minor kind."

The officers of the court had seated themselves again and were all watching the law officer, who was flipping quickly through his own books. He finally emerged with a smile and a reference of his own.

"All of that is correct, Captain, except for the fact that the accused here *did* absent himself from his assigned station, the Transit Rankers' Center, and was at large upon the planet Helior."

"All of which is correct, sir," O'Brien said, whipping out yet another volume and waving it over his head. "But in Dragsted versus the Imperial Navy Billeting Corps, Helior, 8832, it was agreed that for purposes of legal definition the planet Helior was to be defined as the City of Helior, and the City of Helior was to be defined as the planet Helior."

"All of which is undoubtedly true," the president interrupted, "but totally beside the point. They have no bearing upon the present case and I'll ask you to snap it up, Captain, because I have a golf appointment."

"You can tee off in ten minutes, sir, if you allow both those precedents to stand. I then introduce one last item, a document drawn up by Fleet Admiral Marmoset—"

"Why, that's me!" the president gasped.

"—at the onset of hostilities with the Chingers when the City of Helior was declared under martial law and considered to be a single military establishment. I therefore submit that the accused is innocent of the charge of desertion since he never left this planet, therefore he never left this city, therefore he never left his post of duty."

A heavy silence fell and was finally broken by the president's worried voice as he turned to the law officer. "Is what this bowb says true, Pablo? Can't we shoot the guy?"

The law officer was sweating as he searched feverishly

through his law books, then finally pushed them from him and answered in a bitter voice. "True enough and no way out of it. This Arabic-Jewish-Irish con man has got us by the short hair. The accused is innocent of the charges."

"No execution . . . ?" one of the court officers asked in a high, querulous voice, and another, older one dropped his head onto his arms and began to sob.

"Well he's not getting off that easily," the president said, scowling at Bill. "If the accused was on this post for the last year then he should have been on duty. And during that year he must have slept. Which means he *slept on duty*. Therefore I sentence him to hard labor in military prison for one year and one day and order that he be reduced in rank to Fuse Tender Seventh Class. Tear off his stripes and take him away; I have to get to the golf course.

II

The transit stockade was a makeshift building of plastic sheets bolted to bent aluminum frames and was in the center of a large quadrangle. MPs with bayoneted atomrifles marched around the perimeter of the six electrified barbed-wire fences. The multiple gates were opened by remote control, and Bill was dragged through them by the handcuff robot that had brought him here. This debased machine was a squat and heavy cube as high as his knee that ran on clanking treads and from the top of which projected a steel bar with heavy handcuffs fastened to the end. Bill was on the end of the handcuffs. Escape was impossible, because if any attempt was made to force the cuffs the robot sadistically exploded a pee-wee atom bomb it had in its guts and blew up itself and the escaping prisoner, as well as anyone else in the vicinity. Once inside the compound the robot stopped and did not protest when the guard sergeant unlocked the cuffs. As soon as its prisoner was freed the machine rolled into its kennel and vanished.

"All right, wise guy, you're in *my* charge now, and dat means trouble for you," the sergeant snapped at Bill. He had a shaven head, a wide and scar-covered jaw, small, close-set eyes in which there flickered the guttering candle of stupidity.

Bill narrowed his own eyes to slits and slowly raised his good left-right arm, flexing the biceps. Tembo's muscle swelled and split the thin prison fatigue jacket with a harsh, ripping sound. Then Bill pointed to the ribbon of the Purple Dart which he had pinned to his chest.

"Do you know how I got that?" he asked in a grim and toneless voice. "I got that by killing thirteen Chingers single-handed in a pillbox I had been sent into. I got into this stockade here because after killing the Chingers I came back and killed the sergeant who sent me in there. Now—what did you say about trouble, Sergeant?"

"You don't give me no trouble I don't give you no trouble," the guard sergeant squeaked as he skittered away. "You're in cell 13, in there, right upstairs . . ." He stopped suddenly and began to chew all the fingernails on one hand at the same time, with a nibbling-crunching sound. Bill gave him a long glower for good measure, then turned and went slowly into the building.

The door to number 13 stood open, and Bill looked in at the narrow cell dimly lit by the light that filtered through the translucent plastic walls. The double-decker bunk took up almost all of the space, leaving only a narrow passage at one side. Two sagging shelves were bolted to the far wall and, along with the stenciled message BE CLEAN NOT OBSCENE— DIRTY TALK HELPS THE ENEMY!, made up the complete furnishings. A small man with a pointed face and beady eyes lay on the bottom bunk looking intently at Bill. Bill looked right back and frowned.

"Come in, Sarge," the little man said as he scuttled up the support into the upper bunk. "I been saving the lower for you, yes I have. The name is Blackey, and I'm doing ten months for telling a second looey to blow it out . . ."

He ended the sentence with a slight questioning note that Bill ignored. Bill's feet hurt. He kicked off the purple boots and stretched out on the sack. Blackey's head popped over the edge of the upper bunk, not unlike a rodent peering out the landscape. "It's a long time to chow—how's about a Dobbin-burger?" A hand appeared next to the head and slipped a shiny package down to Bill.

After looking it over suspiciously Bill pulled the sealing string on the end of the plastic bag. As soon as the air rushed in and hit the combustible lining the burger started to smoke and within three seconds was steaming hot. Lifting the bun Bill squirted ketchup in from the little sack at the other end of the bag, then took a suspicious bite. It was rich, juicy horse.

"This old gray mare sure tastes like it used to be," Bill said, talking with his mouth full. "How did you ever smuggle this into the stockade?"

Blackey grinned and produced a broad stage wink. "Contacts. They bring it in to me, all I gotta do is ask. I didn't catch the name . . . ?"

"Bill." Food had soothed his ruffled temper. "A year and a day for sleeping on duty. I would have been shot for desertion, but I had a good lawyer. That was a good burger, too bad there's nothing to wash it down with."

Blackey produced a small bottle labeled Cough Syrup and passed it to Bill. "Specially mixed for me by a friend in the medics. Half grain alcohol and half ether."

"Zoingg!" Bill said, dashing the tears from his eyes after draining half the bottle. He felt almost at peace with the world. You're a good buddy to have around, Blackey."

"You can say that again," Blackey told him earnestly. "It never hurts to have a buddy, not in the troopers, the army, the navy, anywheres. Ask old Blackey, he knows. You got muscles, Bill?"

Bill lazily flexed Tembo's muscles for him.

"That's what I like to see," Blackey said in admiration. "With your muscles and my brain we can get along fine . . ."

"I have a brain too!"

"Relax it! Give it a break, while I do the thinking. I seen service in more armies than you got days in the troopers. I got my first Purple Heart serving with Hannibal, there's the

155

scar right there." He pointed to a white arc on the back of his hand. "But I picked him for a loser and switched to Romulus and Remus' boys while there was still time. I been learning ever since, and I always land on my feet. I saw which way the wind was blowing and ate some laundry soap and got the trots the morning of Waterloo, and I missed but nothing, I tell you. I saw the same kind of thing shaping up at the Somme—or was it Ypres?—I forget some of them old names now, and chewed a cigarette and put it into my armpit, you get a fever that way, and missed that show too. There's always an angle to figure I always say."

"I never heard of those battles. Fighting the Chingers?"

"No, earlier than that, a lot earlier than that. Wars and wars ago."

"That makes you pretty old, Blackey. You don't look pretty old."

"I am pretty old, but I don't tell people usually because they give me the laugh. But I remember the pyramids being built, and I remember what lousy chow the Assyrian army had, and the time we took over Wug's mob when they tried to get into our cave, rolled rocks down on them."

"Sounds like a lot of bowb," Bill said lazily, draining the bottle.

"Yeah, that's what everybody says, so I don't tell the old stories any more. They don't even believe me when I show them my good-luck piece." He held out a little white triangle with a ragged edge. "Tooth from a pterodactyl. Knocked it down myself with a stone from a sling I had just invented . . ."

"Looks like a hunk of plastic."

"See what I mean? So I don't tell the old stories any more. Just keep re-enlisting and drifting with the tide . . ."

Bill sat up and gaped. "Re-enlist! Why, that's suicide . . ."

"Safe as houses. Safest place during the war is in the army.

The jerks in the front lines get their heads shot off, the civilians at home get their heads blown off. Guys in between safe as houses. It takes thirty, fifty, maybe seventy guys in the middle to supply every guy in the line. Once you learn to be a file clerk you're safe. Who ever heard of them shooting at a file clerk? I'm a great file clerk. But that's just in wartime. Peacetime, whenever they make a mistake and there is peace for awhile, it's better to be in the combat troops. Better food, longer leaves, nothing much to do. Travel a lot."

"So what happens when the war starts?"

"I know 735 different ways to get into the hospitals."

"Will you teach me a couple?"

"Anything for a buddy, Bill. I'll show you tonight, after they bring the chow around. And the guard what brings the chow is being difficult about a little favor I asked him. Boy, I wish he had a broken arm!"

"Which arm?" Bill cracked his knuckles with a loud crunch.

"Dealer's choice."

The Plastichouse Stockade was a transient center where prisoners were kept on the way from somewhere to elsewhere. It was an easy, relaxed life enjoyed by both guards and inmates with nothing to disturb the even tenor of the days. There had been one new guard, a real eager type fresh in from the National Territorial Guard, but he had had an accident while serving the meals and had broken his arm. Even the other guards were glad to see him go. About once a week Blackey would be taken away under armed guard to the Base Records Section where he was forging new records for a light colonel who was very active in the black market and wanted to make millionaire before he retired. While working on the records Blackey saw to it that the stockade guards received undeserved promotions, extra leave time, and cash bonuses for nonexistent medals. As a result Bill and Blackey ate and drank very well and grew fat. It was as peaceful as could possibly be until the morning after a session in the records section when Blackey returned and woke Bill up.

"Good news," he said. "We're shipping out."

"What's good about that?" Bill asked, surly at being disturbed and still half-stoned from the previous evening's drinking bout. "I like it here."

"It's going to get too hot for us soon. The colonel is giving me the eye and a very funny look, and I think he is going to have us shipped to the other end of the galaxy, where there is heavy fighting. But he's not going to do anything until next week after I finish the books for him, so I had secret orders cut for us *this* week sending us to Tabes Dorsalis where the cement mines are."

"The Dust World!" Bill shouted hoarsely, and picked Blackey up by the throat and shook him. "A world-wide cement mine where men die of silicosis in hours. Hellhole of the universe . . ."

Blackey wriggled free and scuttled to the other end of the cell.

"Hold it!" he gasped. "Don't go off half cocked. Close the cover on your priming pan and keep your powder dry! Do you think I would ship us to a place like that? That's just the way it is on the TV shows, but I got the inside dope. If you work in the cement mines, roger, it ain't so good. But they got one tremendous base section there with a lot of clerical help, and they use trustees in the motor pool, since there aren't enough troops there. While I was working on the records I changed your MS from fuse tender, which is a suicide job, to driver, and here is your driver's license with qualifications on everything from monocycle to atomic 89-

ton tank. So we get us some soft jobs, and besides, the whole base is air-conditioned."

"It was kind of nice here," Bill said, scowling at the plastic card that certified to his aptitude in chauffeuring a number of strange vehicles, most of which he had never seen.

"They come, they go, they're all the same," Blackey said, packing a small toilet kit.

They began to realize that something was wrong when the column of prisoners was shackled then chained together with neckcuffs and leg irons and prodded into the transport spacer by a platoon of combat MPs. "Move along!" they shouted. "You'll have plenty of time to relax when we got to Tabes Dorsalgia."

"Where are we going?" Bill gasped.

"You heard me, snap it bowb."

"You told me Tabes Dorsalis," Bill snarled at Blackey who was ahead of him in the chain. "Tabes Dorsalgia is the base on Veneria where all the fighting is going on—we're heading for combat!"

"A little slip of the pen," Blackey sighed. "You can't win them all."

He dodged the kick Bill swung at him, then waited patiently while the MPs beat Bill senseless with their clubs and dragged him aboard the ship.

III

Veneria . . . a fog-shrouded world of untold horrors, creeping in its orbit around the ghoulish green star Hernia like some repellent heavenly trespasser newly rose from the nethermost pit. What secrets lie beneath the eternal mists? What nameless monsters undulate and gibber in its dank tarns and bottomless black lagoons? Faced by the unspeakable terrors of this planet men go mad rather than face up to the faceless. Veneria . . . swamp world, the lair of the hideous and unimaginable Venians . . .

It was hot and it was damp and it stank. The wood of the newly constructed barracks was already soft and rotting away. You took your shoes off, and before they hit the floor fungus was growing out of them. Once inside the compound their chains were removed, since there was no place for labor-camp prisoners to escape to, and Bill wheeled around looking for Blackey, the fingers of Tembo's arm snapping like hungry jaws. Then he remembered that Blackey had spoken to one of the guards as they were leaving the ship, had slipped him something, and a little while later had been unlocked from the line and led away. By now he would be running the file section and by tomorrow he would be living in the nurses's quarters. Bill sighed, let the whole thing slip out of his mind and vanish, since it was just one more antagonistic factor that he had no control over, and dropped down onto the nearest bunk. Instantly a vine flashed up from a crack in the floor, whipped four times around the bunk lashing him securely to it, then plunged tendrils into his leg and began to drink his blood.

"Grrrrk . . . !" Bill croaked against the pressure of a green loop that tightened around his throat.

"Never lie down without you got a knife in your hand," a thin, yellowish sergeant said as he passed by, and severed the vine, with his own knife, where it emerged from the floor-boards.

"Thanks, Sarge," Bill said, stripping off the coils and throwing them out the window.

The sergeant suddenly began vibrating like a plucked string and dropped onto the foot of Bill's bunk. "P-pocket . . . shirt . . . p-p-pills . . ." he stuttered through chattering teeth. Bill pulled a plastic box of pills out of the sergeant's pocket and forced some of them into his mouth. The vibrations stopped, and the man sagged back against the wall, gaunter and yellower and streaming with sweat.

"Jaundice and swamp fever and galloping filariasis, never know when an attack will hit me, that's why they can't send me back to combat, I can't hold a gun. Me, Master Sergeant Ferkel, the best damned flamethrower in Kirjassoff's Kut-throats, and they have me playing nursemaid in a prison labor camp. So you think that bugs me? It does not bug me, it makes me happy, and the only thing that would make me happier would be shipping off this cesspool-planet at once."

"Do you think alcohol will hurt your condition?" Bill asked, passing over a bottle of cough syrup. "It's kind of rough here?"

"Not only won't hurt it, but it will . . ." There was a deep gurgling, and when the sergeant spoke again he was hoarser but stronger. "Rough is not the word for it. Fighting the Chingers is bad enough, but on this planet they have the natives, the Venians, on their side. These Venians look like moldy newts, and they got just maybe enough I.Q. to hold a gun and pull the trigger, but it is *their* planet and they are but murder out there in the swamps. They hide under the mud and they swim under the water and they swing from the trees and the whole planet is thick with them. They got no sources of supply, no army divisions, no organizations, they just fight. If one dies the others eat him. If one is wounded in the leg the others eat the leg and he grows a new one. If one of them runs out of ammunition or poison darts or whatever he just swims back a hundred miles to base, loads up, and back to battle. We have been fighting here for three years, and we now control one hundred square miles of territory."

"A hundred, that sounds like a lot."

"Just to a stupid bowb like you. That is ten miles by ten miles, and maybe about two square miles more than we captured in the first landings."

There was the squish-thud of tired feet, and weary, mud-soaked men began to drag into the barracks. Sergeant Ferkel hauled himself to his feet and blew a long blast on his whistle.

"All right you new men, now hear this. You have all been assigned to B squad, which is now assembling in the compound, which squad will now march out into the swamp and finish the job these shagged creeps from A squad began this morning. You will do a good day's work out there. I am not going to appeal to your sense of loyalty, your honor or your sense of duty . . ." Ferkel whipped out his atomic pistol and blew a hole in the ceiling through which rain began to drip. "I am only going to appeal to your urge to survive, because any man shirking, goofing off, or not pulling his own weight will personally be shot dead by me. Now get out." With his bared teeth and shaking hands he looked sick enough and mean enough and mad enough to do it. Bill and the rest of B squad rushed out into the rain and formed ranks.

"Pick up da axes, pick up da picks, get the uranium out," the corporal of the armed guard snarled as they squelched through the mud toward the gate. The labor squad, carrying their tools, stayed in the center, while the armed guard walked on the outside. The guard wasn't there to stop the prisoners from escaping but to give some measure of protection from the enemy. They dragged slowly down the road of felled trees that wound through the swamp. There was a sudden whistling overhead, and heavy transports flashed by.

"We're in luck today," one of the older prisoners said, "they're sending in the heavy infantry again. I didn't know they had any left."

"You mean they'll capture more territory?" Bill asked.

"Naw, all they'll get is dead. But while they're getting butchered some of the pressure will be off of us, and we can maybe work without losing too many men."

Without orders they all stopped to watch as the heavy infantry fell like rain into the swamps ahead—and vanished just as easily as raindrops. Every once in awhile there would be a boom and flash as a teensie A-bomb went off, which probably atomized a few Venians, but there were billions more of the enemy just waiting to rush in. Small arms crackled in the distance, and grenades boomed. Then over the trees they saw a bobbing, bouncing figure approach. It was a heavy infantryman in his armored suit and gasproof helmet, A-bombs and grenades strapped to him, a regular walking armory. Or rather hopping armory, since he would have had trouble walking on a paved street with the weight of junk hung about him, so he therefore moved by jumping, using two reaction rockets, one bolted to each hip. His hops were getting lower and lower as he came near. He landed fifty yards away and slowly sank to his waist in the swamp, his rockets hissing as they touched the water. Then he hopped again, much shorter this time, the rockets fizzling and popping, and he threw his helmet open in the air.

"Hey, guys," he called. "The dirty Chingers got my fuel

tank. My rockets are almost out, I can't hop much more. Give a buddy a hand will you . . ." He hit the water with a splash.

"Get outta the monkey suit and we'll pull you in," the guard corporal called.

"Are you nuts!" the soldier shouted. "It takes an hour to get into and outta this thing." He triggered his rockets, but they just went *pffft*, and he rose about a foot in the water, then dropped back. "The fuel's gone! Help me you bastards! What's this, bowb-your-buddy week . . ." he shouted as he sank. Then his head went under, and there were a few bubbles and nothing else.

"It's always bowb-your-buddy week," the corporal said. "Get the column moving!" he ordered, and they shuffled forward. "Them suits weigh three thousand pounds. Go down like a rock."

If this was a quiet day, Bill didn't want to see a busy one. Since the entire planet of Veneria was a swamp no advances could be made until a road was built. Individual soldiers might penetrate a bit ahead of the road, but for equipment or supplies or even heavily armed men a road was necessary. Therefore the labor corps was building a road of felled trees. At the front.

Bursts from atomrifles steamed in the water around them, and the poison darts were as thick as falling leaves. The firing and sniping on both sides was constant while the prisoners cut down trees and trimmed and lashed them together to push the road forward another few inches. Bill trimmed and chopped and tried to ignore the screams and falling bodies until it began to grow dark. The squad, now a good deal smaller, made their return march in the dusk.

"We pushed it ahead at least thirty yards this afternoon," Bill said to the old prisoner marching at his side.

"Don't mean nothing, Venians swim up in the night and take the logs away."

Bill instantly made his mind up to get out of there.

"Got any more of that joyjuice?" Sergeant Ferkel asked when Bill dropped onto his bunk and began to scrape some of the mud from his boots with the blade of his knife. Bill took a quick slash at a plant coming up through the floorboards before he answered.

"Do you think you could spare me a moment to give me some advice, Sergeant?"

"I am a flowing fountain of advice once my throat is lubricated."

Bill dug a bottle out of his pocket. "How do you get out of this outfit?" he asked.

"You get killed," the sergeant told him as he raised the bottle to his lips. Bill snatched it out of his hand.

"That I know without your help," he snarled.

"Well that's all you gonna know without my help," the sergeant snarled back.

Their noses were touching and they growled at each other deep in their throats. Having proven just where they stood and just how tough they both were they relaxed, and Sergeant Ferkel leaned back while Bill sighed and passed him the bottle.

"How's about a job in the orderly room?" Bill asked.

"We don't have an orderly room. We don't have any records. Everyone sent here gets killed sooner or later, so who cares exactly when."

"What about getting wounded?"

"Get sent to the hospital, get well, get sent back here."

"The only thing left to do is mutiny!" Bill shouted.

"Didn't work last four times we tried it. They just pulled the supply ships out and didn't give us any food until we agreed to start fighting again. Wrong chemistry here, all the food on this planet is pure poison for our metabolisms. We had a couple of guys prove it the hard way. Any mutiny that is going to succeed has to grab enough ships first so we can get off-planet. If you got any good ideas about that I'll put you in touch with the Permanent Mutiny Committee."

"Isn't there *any* way to get out?"

"I anshered that firsht," Ferkel told him, and fell over stone drunk.

"I'll see for myself," Bill said as he slid the sergeant's pistol from his holster, then slipped out the back door.

Armored floodlights lit up the forward positions facing the enemy, and Bill went in the opposite direction, toward the distant white flares of landing rockets. Barracks and warehouses were dotted about on the boggy ground, but Bill stayed clear of them since they were all guarded, and the guards had itchy trigger fingers. They fired at anything they saw, anything they heard, and if they didn't see or hear anything they fired once in a while anyway just to keep their morale up. Lights were burning brightly ahead, and Bill crawled forward on his stomach to peer from behind a rank growth at a tall, floodlighted fence of barbed wire that stretched out of sight in both directions.

A burst from an atomic rifle burned a hole in the mud about a yard behind him, and a searchlight swung over, catching him full in its glare.

"Greetings from your commanding officer," an amplified voice thundered from loudspeakers on the fence. "This is a recorded announcement. You are now attempting to leave the combat zone and enter the restricted headquarters zone. This is forbidden. Your presence has been detected by automatic machinery, and these same devices now have a number of guns trained upon you. They will fire in sixty seconds if you do not leave. Be patriotic, man! Do your duty. Death to the Chingers! Fifty-five seconds. Would you like your mother to know that her boy is a coward? Fifty seconds. Your Emperor has invested a lot of money in your training—is this the way that you repay him? Forty-five seconds . . ."

Bill cursed and shot up the nearest loudspeaker, but the voice continued from others down the length of the fence. He turned and went back the way he had come.

As he neared his barracks, skirting the front line to avoid the fire from the nervous guards in the buildings, all the lights went out. At the same time gunfire and bomb explosions broke out on every side.

IV

Something slithered close by in the mud and Bill's trigger finger spontaneously contracted and he shot it. In the brief atomic flare he saw the smoking remains of a dead Venian, as well as an unusually large number of live Venians squelching to the attack. Bill dived aside instantly, so that their return fire missed him, and fled in the opposite direction. His only thought was to save his skin, and this he did by getting as far from the firing and the attacking enemy as he could. That this direction happened to be into the trackless swamp he did not consider at the time. *Survive*, his shivering little ego screamed, and he ran on.

Running became difficult when the ground turned to mud, and even more difficult when the mud gave way to open water. After paddling desperately for an interminable length of time Bill came to more mud. The first hysteria had now passed, the firing was only a dull rumble in the distance, and he was exhausted. He dropped onto the mudbank and instantly sharp teeth sank deep into his buttocks. Screaming hoarsely, he ran on until he ran into a tree. He wasn't going fast enough to hurt himself, and the feel of rough bark under his fingers brought out all of his eoanthropic survival instincts: he climbed. High up there were two branches that forked out from the trunk, and he wedged himself into the crotch, back to the solid wood and gun pointed straight ahead and ready. Nothing bothered him now. The night sounds grew dim and distant, the blackness was complete, and within a few minutes his head started to nod. He dragged it back up a few times, blinked about at nothing, then finally slept.

It was the first gray light of dawn when he opened his gummy eyes and blinked around. There was a little lizard perched on a nearby branch watching him with jewel-like eyes.

"Gee—you were really sacked out," the Chinger said.

Bill's shot tore a smoking scar in the top of the branch, then the Chinger swung back up from underneath and meticulously wiped bits of ash from his paws.

"Easy on the trigger, Bill," it said. "Gee—I could have killed you anytime during the night if I had wanted to."

"I know you," Bill said hoarsely. "You're Eager Beager, aren't you?"

"Gee—this is just like old home week, isn't it?" A centipede was scuttling by, and Eager Beager the Chinger grabbed it up with three of his arms and began pulling off legs with his fourth and eating them. "I recognized you Bill, and wanted to talk to you. I have been feeling bad ever since I called you a stoolie, that wasn't right of me. You were only doing your duty when you turned me in. You wouldn't like to tell me how you recognized me, would you . . . ?" he asked, and winked slyly.

"Why don't you bowb off, Jack?" Bill growled, and groped in his pocket for a bottle of cough syrup. Eager Chinger sighed.

"Well, I suppose I can't expect you to betray anything of military importance, but I hope you will answer a few questions for me." He discarded the delimbed corpse and groped about in his marsupial pouch and produced a tablet and tiny writing instrument. "You must realize that spying is not my chosen occupation, but rather I was dragooned into it through my speciality, which is exopology—perhaps you have heard of this discipline . . . ?"

169

"We had an orientation lecture once, an exopologist, all he could talk about was alien creeps and things."

"Yes—well, that roughly sums it up. The science of the study of alien life forms, and of course to us you homo sapiens are an alien form . . ." He scuttled halfway around the branch when Bill raised his gun.

"Watch that kind of talk, bowb!"

"Sorry, just my manner of speaking. To put it briefly, since I specialized in the study of your species I was sent out as a spy, reluctantly, but that is the sort of sacrifice one makes during wartime. However, seeing you here reminded me that there are a number of questions and problems still unanswered that I would appreciate your help on, purely in the matter of science of course."

"Like what?" Bill asked suspiciously, draining the bottle and flinging it away into the jungle.

"Well—gee—to begin simply, how do you feel about us Chingers?"

"Death to all Chingers!" The little pen flew over the tablet.

"But you have been *taught* to say that. How did you feel before you entered the service?"

"Didn't give a damn about Chingers." Out of the corner of his eye Bill was watching a suspicious movement of the leaves in the tree above.

"Fine! Then could you explain to me just who it is that hates us Chingers and wants to fight a war of extermination?"

"Nobody really hates Chingers, I guess. It's just that there is no one else around to fight a war with, so we fight with you." The moving leaves had parted and a great, smooth head with slitted eyes peered down.

"I knew it! And that brings me to my really important question. Why *do* you homo sapiens like to fight wars?"

Bill's hand tightened on his gun as the monstrous head

dropped silently down from the leaves behind Eager Chinger Beager; it was attached to a foot-thick and apparently endless serpent body.

"Fight wars? I don't know," Bill said, distracted by the soundless approach of the giant snake. "I guess because we like to, there doesn't seem to be any other reason."

"You *like* to!" the Chinger squeaked, hopping up and down with excitement. "No civilized race could *like* wars, death, killing, maiming, rape, torture, pain, to name just a few of the concomitant factors. Your race can't be civilized!"

The snake struck like lightning, and Eager Beager Chinger vanished down its spine-covered throat with only the slightest of muffled squeals.

"Yeah . . . I guess we're just not civilized," Bill said, gun ready, but the snake kept going on down. At least fifty yards of it slithered by before the tail flipped past and it was out of sight. "Serves the damn spy right," Bill grunted happily, and pulled himself to his feet.

Once on the ground Bill began to realize just how bad a spot he was in. The damp swamp had swallowed up any marks of his passage from the night before and he hadn't the slightest idea in which direction the battle area lay. The sun was just a general illumination behind the layers of fog and cloud, and he felt a sudden chill as he realized how small were his chances of finding his way back. The invasion area, just ten miles to a side, made a microscopic pinprick in the hide of this planet. Yet if he didn't find it he was as good as dead. And if he just stayed here he would die, so, picking what looked like the most likely direction, he started off.

"I'm pooped," he said, and was. A few hours of dragging through the swamps had done nothing except weaken his muscles, fill his skin with insect bites, drain a quart or two of blood into the ubiquitous leeches, and deplete the charge in his gun as he killed a dozen or so of the local life forms that wanted him for breakfast. He was also hungry and thirsty. And still lost.

The rest of the day just recapitulated the morning, so that when the sky began to darken he was close to exhaustion, and his supply of cough medicine was gone. He was very hungry when he climbed a tree to find a spot to rest for the night, and he plucked a luscious-looking red fruit.

"Supposed to be poison." He looked at it suspiciously, then smelled it. It smelled fine. He threw it away.

In the morning he was much hungrier. "Should I put the barrel of the gun in my mouth and blow my head off?" he asked himself, weighing the atomic pistol in his hand. "Plenty of time for that yet. Plenty of things can still happen." Yet he didn't really believe it when he heard voices coming through the jungle toward him, human voices. He settled behind the limb and aimed his gun in that direction.

The voices grew louder, then a clanking and rattling. An armed Venian scuttled under the tree, but Bill held his fire as other figures loomed out of the fog. It was a long file of human prisoners wearing the neck irons used to bring Bill and the others to the labor camp, all joined together by a long chain that connected the neck irons. Each of the men was carrying a large box on his head. Bill let them stumble by underneath and kept a careful count of the Venian guards. There were five in all with a sixth bringing up the rear, and when this one had passed underneath the tree Bill dropped straight down on him, braining him with his heavy boots. The Venian was armed with a Chinger-made copy of a standard atomic rifle, and Bill smiled wickedly as he hefted its familiar weight. After sticking the pistol into his waistband he crept after the column, rifle ready. He managed to kill the fifth guard by walking up behind him and catching him in the back of the neck with the rifle butt. The last two troopers in the file saw this but had enough brains to be quiet as he crept up on number four. Some stir among the prisoners or a chance sound warned this guard and he turned about, raising his rifle. There was no chance now to kill him silently, so Bill burned his head off and ran as fast as he could toward the head of the column. There was a shocked silence when the blast of the rifle echoed through the fog and Bill filled it with a shout.

"Hit the dirt—FAST!"

The soldiers dived into the mud and Bill held his atomic rifle at his waist as he ran, fanning it back and forth before him like a water hose and holding down the trigger on full automatic. A continuous blast of fire poured out a yard above the ground and he squirted it in an arc before him. There were shouts and screams in the fog, and then the charge in the rifle was exhausted. Bill threw it from him and drew the pistol. Two of the remaining guards were down, and the last one was wounded and got off a single badly aimed shot before Bill burned him too.

"Not bad," he said, stopping and panting. "Six out of six."

There were low moans coming from the line of prisoners, and Bill curled his lip in disgust at the three men who hadn't dropped at his shouted command.

"What's the matter?" he asked, stirring one with his foot, "never been in combat before?" But this one didn't answer because he was charred dead.

"Never . . ." the next one answered, gasping in pain. "Get the corpsman, I'm wounded, there's one ahead in the line. Oh, oh, why did I ever leave the *Chris Keeler!* Medic . . ."

Bill frowned at the three gold balls of a fourth lieutenant on the man's collar, then bent and scraped some mud from his face. "You! The laundry officer!" he shouted in outraged anger, raising his gun to finish the job.

"Not I!" the lieutenant moaned, recognizing Bill at last.

"The laundry officer is gone, flushed down the drain! This is I, your friendly local pastor, bringing you the blessings of Ahura Mazdah, my son, and have you been reading the Avesta every day before going to sleep . . ."

"Bah!" Bill snarled. He couldn't shoot him now, and he walked over to the third wounded man.

"Hello Bill . . ." a weak voice said. "I guess the old reflexes are slowing down . . . I can't blame you for shooting me, I should have hit the dirt like the others . . ."

"You're damn right you should have," Bill said looking down at the familiar, loathed, tusked face. "You're dying, Deathwish, you've bought it."

"I know," Deathwish said, and coughed. His eyes were closed.

"Wrap this line in a circle," Bill shouted. "I want the medic up here." The chain of prisoners curved around, and they watched as the medic examined the casualties.

"A bandage on the looie's arm takes care of him," he said. "Just superficial burns. But the big guy with the fangs has bought it."

"Can you keep him alive?" Bill asked.

"For awhile, no telling how long."

"Keep him alive." Bill looked around at the circle of prisoners. "Any way to get those neck irons off?" he asked.

"Not without the keys," a burly infantry sergeant answered, "and the lizards never brought them. We'll have to wear them until we get back. How come you risked your neck saving us?" he asked suspiciously.

"Who wanted to save you?" Bill sneered. "I was hungry and I figured that must be food you were carrying."

"Yeah, it is," the sergeant said, looking relieved. "I can understand now why you took the chance."

Bill broke open a can of rations and stuffed his face.

V

The dead man was cut from his position in the line, and the two men, one in front and one in back of the wounded Deathwish, wanted to do the same with him. Bill reasoned with them, explained the only human thing to do was to carry their buddy, and they agreed with him when he threatened to burn their legs off if they didn't. While the chained men were eating, Bill cut two flexible poles and made a stretcher by slipping three donated uniform jackets over them. He gave the captured rifles to the burly sergeant and the most likely looking combat veterans, keeping one for himself.

"Any chance of getting back?" Bill asked the sergeant, who was carefully wiping the moisture from his gun.

"Maybe. We can backtrack the way we come, easy enough to follow the trail after everyone dragged through. Keep an eye peeled for Venians, get them before they can spread the word about us. When we get in earshot of the fighting we try and find a quiet area—then break through. A fifty-fifty chance."

"Those are better odds for all of us than they were about an hour ago."

"You're telling me. But they get worse the longer we hang around here."

"Let's get moving."

Following the track was even easier than Bill had thought, and by early afternoon they heard the first signs of firing, a dim rumble in the distance. The only Venian they had seen had been instantly killed. Bill halted the march.

"Eat as much as you want, then dump the food," he said.

"Pass that on. We'll be moving fast soon." He went to see how Deathwish was getting on.

"Badly—" Deathwish gasped, his face white as paper. "This is it, Bill . . . I know it . . . I've terrorized my last recruit . . . stood on my last pay line . . . had my last short-arm . . . so long—Bill . . . you're a good buddy . . . taking care of me like this . . ."

"Glad you think so, Deathwish, and maybe you'd like to do me a favor." He dug in the dying man's pockets until he found his noncom's notebook, then opened it and scrawled on one of the blank pages. "How would you like to sign this, just for old time's sake—Deathwish?"

The big jaw lay slack, the evil red eyes open and staring.

"The dirty bowb's gone and died on me," Bill said disgustedly. After pondering for a moment he dribbled some ink from the pen onto the ball of Deathwish's thumb and pressed it to the paper to make a print.

"Medic!" he shouted, and the line of men curled around so the medic could come back. "How does he look to you?"

"Dead as a herring," the corpsman said after his professional examination.

"Just before he died he left me his tusks in his will, written right down here, see? These are real vat-grown tusks and cost a lot. Can they be transplanted?"

"Sure, as long as you get them cut out and deep froze inside the next twelve hours."

"No problem with that, we'll just carry the body back with us." He stared hard at the two stretcher bearers and fingered his gun, and they had no complaints. "Get that lieutenant up here."

"Chaplain," Bill said, holding out the sheet from the notebook, "I would like an officer's signature on this. Just before he died this trooper here dictated his will, but was too weak to sign it, so he put his thumbprint on it. Now you write below it that you saw him thumbprint it and it is all affirm and legal-like, then sign your name."

"But—I couldn't do that, my son. I did not see the deceased print the will and Glmmpf . . ."

He said Glmmpf because Bill had poked the barrel of the atomic pistol into his mouth and was rotating it, his finger quivering on the trigger.

"Shoot," the infantry sergeant said, and three of the men who could see what was going on were clapping. Bill slowly withdrew the pistol.

"I shall be happy to help," the chaplain said, grabbing for the pen.

Bill read the document, grunted in satisfaction, then went over and squatted down next to the medic. "You from the hospital?" he asked.

"You can say that again, and if I ever get back into the hospital I ain't never going out of it again. It was just my luck to be out picking up combat casualties when the raid hit."

"I hear that they aren't shipping any wounded out. Just putting them back into shape and sending them back into the line."

"You heard right. This is going to be a hard war to live through."

"But *some* of them must be wounded too badly to send back into action," Bill insisted.

"The miracles of modern medicine," the medic said indistinctly as he worried a cake of dehydrated luncheon meat. "Either you die or you're back in the line in a couple of weeks."

"Maybe a guy gets his arm blown off?"

"They got an icebox full of old arms. Sew a new one on and bango, right back into the line."

"What about a foot?" Bill asked, worried.

"That's right—I forgot! They got a foot shortage. So many

guys lying around without feet that they're running out of bed space. They were just starting to ship some of them off-planet when I left."

"You got any pain pills?" Bill asked, changing the subject. The medic dug out a white bottle.

"Three of these and you'd laugh while they sawed your head off."

"Give me three."

"If you ever see a guy around what has his foot shot off, you better quick tie something around his leg just over the knee, tight, to cut the blood off."

"Thanks buddy."

"No skin off my nose."

"Let's get moving," the infantry sergeant said. "The quicker we move the better our chances."

Occasional flares from atomic rifles burned through the foliage overhead, and the thud-thud of heavy weapons shook the mud under their feet. They worked along parallel with the firing until it had died down, then stopped. Bill, the only one not chained in the line, crawled ahead to reconnoiter. The enemy lines seemed to be lightly held and he found a spot that looked the best for a breakthrough. Then, before he returned, he dug the heavy cord from his pocket that he had taken from one of the ration boxes. He tied a tourniquet above his right knee and twisted it tight with a stick, then swallowed the three pills. He stayed behind some heavy shrubs when he called to the others.

"Straight ahead, then sharp right before that clump of trees. Let's go—and FAST!"

Bill led the way until the first men could see the lines ahead. Then he called out "What's that?" and ran into the heavy foliage. "Chingers!" he shouted, and sat down with his back to a tree.

He took careful aim with his pistol and blew his right foot off.

"Get moving fast!" he shouted, and heard the crash of the frightened men through the undergrowth. He threw the pistol away, fired at random into the trees a few times, then dragged to his feet. The atomic rifle made a good enough crutch to hobble along on, and he did not have far to go. Two troopers, they must have been new to combat or they would have known better, left the shelter to help him inside.

"Thanks, buddies," he gasped, and sank to the ground. "War sure is hell."

ENVOI

The martial music echoed from the hillside, bouncing back from the rocky ledges and losing itself in the hushed green shadows under the trees. Around the bend, stamping proudly through the dust, came the little parade led by the magnificent form of a one-robot band. Sunlight gleamed on its golden limbs and twinkled from the brazen instruments it worked with such enthusiasm. A small formation of assorted robots rolled and clattered in its wake, and bringing up the rear was the solitary figure of the grizzle-haired recruiting sergeant, striding along strongly, his rows of medals ajingle. Though the road was smooth the sergeant lurched suddenly, stumbling, and cursed with the rich proficiency of years.

"Halt!" he commanded, and while his little company braked to a stop he leaned against the stone wall that bordered the road and rolled up his right pants leg. When he whistled one of the robots trundled quickly over and held out a tool box from which the sergeant took a large screwdriver and tightened one of the bolts in the ankle of his artificial foot. Then he squirted a few drops from an oil can onto the joint and rolled the pants leg back down. When he straightened up he noticed that a robomule was pulling a plow down a furrow in the field beyond the fence, while a husky farm lad guided it.

"Beer!" the sergeant barked, then, "'A Spaceman's Lament.'"

The one-robot band brought forth the gentle melodies of the old song, and by the time the furrow reached the limits of the field there were two dew-frosted steins of beer resting on the fence.

"That's sure pretty music," the plowboy said.

"Join me in a beer," the sergeant said, sprinkling a white powder into it from a packet concealed in his hand.

"Don't mind iffen I do, sure is hotter'n h— out here today."

"Say *hell*, son, I heard the word before."

"Mamma don't like me to cuss. You sure do have long teeth, mister."

The sergeant twanged a tusk. "A big fellow like you should cuss a bit. If you were a trooper you could say *hell*— or even *bowb*—if you wanted to, all the time."

"I don't think I'd want to say anything like *that*." He flushed red under his deep tan. "Thanks for the beer, but I gotta be plowing on now. Mamma said I was to never talk to soldiers."

"Your mamma's right, a dirty, cursing, drinking crew the most of them. Say, would you like to see a picture here of a new model robomule that can run a thousand hours without lubrication?" The sergeant held his hand out behind him, and a robot put a viewer into it.

"Why that sounds nice!" The farm lad raised the viewer to his eyes and looked into it and flushed an even deeper red. "That's no mule, mister, that's a *girl* and her clothes are . . ."

The sergeant reached out swiftly and pressed a button on the top of the viewer. Something went *thunk* inside of it, and the farmer stood rigid and frozen. He did not move or change expression when the sergeant reached out and took the little machine from his paralyzed fingers.

"Take this stylo," the sergeant said, and the other's fingers closed on it. "Now sign this form, right down there where it says RECRUIT'S SIGNATURE . . ." The stylo scratched, and a sudden scream pierced the air.

"My Charlie! What are you doing with my Charlie!" an ancient, gray-haired woman wailed, as she scrambled around the hill.

"Your son is now a trooper for the greater glory of the Emperor," the sergeant said, and waved over the robot tailor.

"No—please—" the woman begged, clutching the sergeant's hand and dribbling tears onto it. "I've lost one son, isn't that enough . . ." she blinked up through the tears, then blinked again. "But you—you're my boy! My Bill come home! Even with those teeth and the scars and one black hand and one white hand and one artificial foot, I can tell; a mother always knows!"

The sergeant frowned down at the woman. "I believe you might be right," he said. "I thought the name Phigerinadon II sounded familiar."

The robot tailor had finished his job. The red paper jacket shone bravely in the sun, the one-molecule-thick boots gleamed. "Fall in," Bill shouted, and the recruit climbed over the wall.

"Billy, Billy . . ." the woman wailed, "this is your little brother Charlie! You wouldn't take your own little brother into the troopers, would you?"

Bill thought about his mother, then he thought about his baby brother Charlie, then he thought of the one month that would be taken off of his enlistment time for every recruit he brought in, and he snapped his answer back instantly.

"Yes," he said.

The music blared, the soldiers marched, the mother cried—as mothers have always done—and the brave little band tramped down the road and over the hill and out of sight into the sunset.

DON'T STOP READING YET!

I hope that I have caught you in time. Just when you thought that you had finished this saga of unrequited passion, alcoholism and that kind of bowb; just when you were about to close the book; just at this historical point of time—I have good news for you.

The saga of Bill, the Galactic Hero, is not quite over yet. You might think it is—but think again. You have watched our hero mature, grow wise with military wisdom, grow stupid again as overindulgence in alcohol corroded his brain cells. You have laughed with him, cried with him, averted your eyes when he stealthily and tumescently sneaked through the back door of Ye Olde Knocking Shop.

But Bill's military career has just begun. In the final part of this book, tastefully titled "Envoi," your Friendly Author let you glimpse a bit of the future, just so you wouldn't feel bad. So you would not think ever-lovable Bill would get blown to pieces, or some such, the very moment after you had closed the book.

No way! Bill may act a little stupid at times and have some pretty repulsive habits—but he is a survivor! Cast your mind back to the last chapter. There he was on a planet of no escape, a deathworld where many arrived and damn few left. To make sure he was one of that elite few he used guts, ingenuity—and a well-aimed gun—to blow his foot off. The rest, as they say, is history.

And you will now have a chance to read that history. Between the time Bill was shlepped offplanet to the foot hospital and the time he became a grizzled Recruiting Sergeant he had many exciting, dangerous, occasionally repulsive, always fascinating adventures.

I have chronicled the first of these in a book with the fetchingly brief title *Bill the Galactic Hero: The Planet of the Robot Slaves.* You will want to read it. I bet that you can already hear the mechanical squeaks of pain as the barbed-wire whips clang down on delicate metal skin!

This book is yours to read. It may be available at the very same retail outlet where you purchased this volume.

And the good news is still coming! The continuing saga of Bill will continue. Develop a habit you won't want to break. Other books are already being written. The future is yours!

Or at least that part of it where the rockets rocket, the Chingers ching, and Bill, the Galactic Hero, limps valiantly toward his destiny.

THE AUTHOR